Spooky Tales & Scary Things
3

Spooky Tales & Scary Things 3

Harry Carpenter

Contents

I BECAME INSANE, WITH LONG INTERVALS OF HORRI-
BLE SANITY.

-EDGAR ALLAN POE

Dedicated to Audrey for putting up with all of my spooky stuff.

Also dedicated to Attral, who never got the chance to see my book or book festival shine. Cereal IS Soup, Birds Arent' Real, but I'm firm on my stance of talented professional wrestlers.

Introduction

Welcome to another installment of *Spooky Tales and Scary Things*! Let me say from the start that it's been a hell of a ride. *Spooky Tales and Scary Things 1* was the second book I ever wrote but the first one of my horror writings. To be writing a third one is near mind-blowing. The series has come a long way, too.

When I set out to write *Spooky Tales and Scary Things*, I wanted to tell short stories about things that happened to me. I've dealt with some wild things in my time, and what better platform to share it on than writing? Writing "The General" and "Demon Dog" were extremely personal and will always hold a place in my heart. A few friends from the era of "The General" still remember the story, the radio situation, and more. Yes, there was even a song about it. No, you can't find it.

When I wrote "Demon Dog," I had such a fun time changing the dynamic from my childhood to that of young Robin and her father. I wrote a lot of my dad into the character of the father, even the *Hokey Smokes*, which the father utters in the story. Changing the character to a girl was also a fun decision, because using the name *Robin* was a nod to my mother, who had wanted to name me *Christopher Robin Carpenter*. I'm glad my classmates only beat me up half as much for being named *Harry*.

"Bathell" was a movie script and not something I experienced. I'd say that was the first deviation I made from the plan of writing about things that revolved around me. I hadn't figured it out yet, but that would ultimately become the formula. In *Spooky Tales and Scary Things 2*, I doubled down on the personal experiences but with a lot more creative flair. I was far more abstract with this one.

I based stories like "Ghost in the Attic" and "The Fall" on something that happened to me, but taken for such a huge spin, they resembled nothing of their non-fiction counterparts, to an extent. With "Father Figure," however, I kept the essence of that story to its roots. It was truly a story for my grandmother and my dad and my uncles.

With the publication of this one, it's the first *Spooky Tales and Scary Things* installment that my grandmother won't get to read. My grandfather passed just after I published the second one. Grandma followed a year later. They both shared many long years on this Earth, and I miss them greatly. They were some of my biggest champions in the family. My grandmother had published a duck-carving book some thirty-plus years ago, too. While she had extremely dated information (such as calling an 800 number to get an ISBN), she gave me a few pointers and foundations that I still implement today.

Second to them is my Uncle Don, whom I have forbade from buying multiple copies of my books at bookstores. While I love the support, others need a chance to buy them too! This gentle dedication isn't enough to express how thankful I am for all their support over the years.

My wife has also been my champion and cheerleader more than she had been in the past. Telling some of the recent stories, she'd raise an eyebrow and say, "Well, that's unique enough." It also helps that a story or two involved her or that our relationship inspired the story, to an extent. It only took her six years to think I'm a real author.

Since publishing the first *Spooky Tales and Scary Things*, I've found myself as a featured author at numerous book signings, comic conventions, and more. It's been a wonderful experience. One thing that never ceases to make me giggle is when someone approaches my table and points to a book and yells, "That was fucking fantastic!" It's even better when someone was on the fence about getting it.

To all of you who read my books throughout the years, and saw the shift in writing style, voice, and more, I thank you for hanging on. I still profess that *Memoirs of a Crazed Mind* is still my best story overall, but I'll one day dethrone it. Maybe this will be the one? Maybe it took three *Spooky Tales and Scary Things* to hit the groove? Who knows?

Finally, I'd like to thank everyone who supported the crazy idea I had three years ago. I tried to vend at a horror book festival in Maryland in 2019. They denied me and said I wasn't *horror enough*. Turns out, they wanted strictly erotica, and that wasn't my thing. I pulled a Futurama's Bender and said, "I'll make my own book festival, with hookers and blackjack!"

Despite my rejection from the event, I buckled down and really put some serious thought into creating my own event—a place where myself and others who write and enjoy horror could unite and share a common passion. FrightReads Book Festival has become successful enough where I even have a hard time selling my own books, which was the entire purpose of its creation. Crazy, right? I couldn't have pulled it off without my crazy friends who supported the idea.

Thanks again to Curmudgeon Books and Capricho's Books for their continued support. I don't think I would have gotten off the ground without you guys. Jeff and Liz were instrumental in giving me the knowledge, confidence, and shelf space to level-up.

For an intro, I could have discussed my spooky inspirations. I could have told a cool ghost story or vented about something that bugged me. Why do that, when you have over a dozen stories ahead? I hope every story is well received, even if they're not truly spooky. Thanks for reading!

~ Harry

The Room

It was extremely dark. That was all I can remember. I don't recall anything before this moment of absolute blackness—a room devoid of light. I squinted my eyes to find any traces of light, possibly a crack in a window or under a door. Nothing. Absolute and complete caliginosity. It was jarring, to say the least.

Worst, to add to my misery, the silence was almost unbearable. This room lacked the faint sounds of running water, passing motorcars, or even the chirping of a lark. Everything had been completely stifled, as if I had suddenly fallen deaf, removing myself from the cacophony of the daily dribble of life. I fear it had not been I, with an ailment of hearing impairment, rather the world who had gone silent. My suspicions were confirmed as I heard the rustling sounds of my body when I shifted slightly.

I repeatedly begged for help. My voice grew hoarser and coarser with each belting of the word. I felt as if no one would come to my aid. No one would dare hear my cries for help or my pleas for assistance. No White Knight was on the horizon to spare me from my torment. Indeed, something more lay ahead of me beyond a dark room, devoid of light and sound.

My hands and feet appeared to be bound, yet I felt no restraints on my limbs. I could barely move my arms and could only just slightly move my feet. I wrestled for a moment to see if my restraints would give, again, feeling none on my body. If only a slight bit of light could illuminate the darkness, I would indeed see what the matter was. I had no concept of time. Everything happened all at once yet not at all. Minutes turned to hours; hours turned to days. The night was day; the day was night. Confusion and fear were all I knew.

I must have passed out again from exhaustion, yet I never felt tired. The blackness of my prison provided no favor to guide me in a time to rest. It was possible that my struggling had recharged my body without me realizing it. I must collect myself to make sense of what had happened to me before my assailants had placed me in this room. They had clearly planned this. It felt all too elaborate for them to have hastily tossed this forth. I assured myself once more that they, whoever *they* were, had designed this.

I believed the stale air was a part of their plan to drive my psychosis further. First, the snuffing of light, followed by the stifling of sounds. The decrepit wet air was only a mere test to see if they could break me; I was sure of it. Every stage of this game had been them testing my mental fortitude, and I was not about to allow my kidnappers to break my will. Not even for one second. I had to maintain my wits. I pulled myself together and realized that I needed to sort out what had brought me here in the first place.

I retraced my steps in memory. I recalled awakening in this room of darkness. What of before? How do I lack any memory of a time before my eyes springing to life in this room? Was the anesthetic powerful enough to drive one to amnesia? There was no feeling of pain. I was capable of some movement, but it was minimal. I centered my thinking on the task at hand—revisiting the past. I must remember how I had ended up here to figure out how to get out.

I pondered deeply. Thoughts churned in my mind. I saw a dock. A fanciful port full of ships and strangers coming and going—a delightful place. The idea of the waves crashing on the shore brought a sense of calmness. Something about the water brought me ease. Was I a sailor? Did I fish for the local village? Who was I? I doubted everything I knew, instead, everything I had forgotten. I needed to sort my thoughts.

Time passed as I cataloged my jumbled thoughts. Perhaps I had wronged a merchant sailor, or maybe *I* was the merchant sailor, captured for his wares. Was I, in fact, a soldier of the sea who the enemy had captured? Was I waiting for my crewmates to rescue me? I speedily scrubbed away those thoughts. I never believed I had the fighting spirit in me. This was a more elaborate prison than I thought pirates would have. Robbers of a ship would just as easily toss the captain into the drink before concocting such a ploy of torture. There had to be more.

I sensed a connection between myself and the water. It was hard for me to comprehend. I knew of motorcars, which concluded I was not from the past. I felt no restraints yet could not move. The air grew more stagnant as my thinking continued. My conundrum perplexed me. I could draw the only simple conclusion, which made more sense by the minute I dared not believe. There was simply no way this was possible. The mere thought was absurd.

I dwelled more on my most recent idea. Although it was nonsensical, it jogged my memory. As I focused, I reawakened memories of my childhood, marriage, and life by the sea. I saw everything once more. I saw the wave crash over me, followed by another. The memory hazed beyond that, yet I briefly recalled sand. Sand and voices. Faces, although blurry, surrounded me.

One voice stood out firmly in the crowd. A woman, who simply cried out to no one, "Dear God, he's dead!"

What's This About?

Oh, man. Where do I begin with this one? How about a super dark fear of mine? Death. Sure, I get it. It's not unique to me. However, it's something my brain sits on and mulls around far too often. It's likely the reason I can write such messed-up stories. "The Room" began as something I wanted to submit to an online publication that had a word limit and was looking for something that was, to quote, "different from the usual." I really felt like this was different.

Several months after I submitted it, they rejected me. Something about *lacking emotion or fear or gore*. For starters, not every horror requires gore. Sure, *Spooky Tales and Scary Things 1* was full of gore. That was what I had been going for. *Spooky Tales and Scary Things 2*? A little different. I was going for a supernatural angle. I also wanted to have the readers connect more with the characters and the situation. So that's where this story came from. More on that.

I contemplated how to describe death from the perspective of someone who didn't know they were dead and buried. For starters, most movies, television programs, and books depict people knowing they are, in fact, dead. They just don't typically remember how they ended up in the predicament. Whether it's a drama or a sitcom, the premise feels the same. They end up in some Heaven (or Hell) type of environment, shenanigans ensue, and life—or rather the afterlife—goes on.

I wanted to stray from that entirely. What if you just retained your conscience, but nothing else? We discussed this on the podcast

Others May Fall. It was a local band whom two of its members discussed life on the road and more. I happened to be the *more*. We had talked about *Spooky Tales and Scary Things 1* when it first came out. We discussed ghost stories, demons, and lore. It all took a dark turn when we asked, "What happens when you die?"

Brian, Joe, Lauren—and perhaps me as well—were all shaken. What you can't take from the audio is our expressions. We discussed the possibility of Heaven and Hell, as well as reincarnation. I decided to be *that guy* and offered, "What if there is nothing?" My suggestion was that we just blip out of existence. We don't reincarnate. Our final destination won't be the pearly gates or the alternative. You just *poof*. Gone.

I then went deeper. As someone who loves science, it both fascinates and terrifies me. I really enjoy documentaries about space, time travel, quantum realms, and the like. None of them offer any peace as to what happens next. My final offering to the OMF Podcast was "What if we just remain in our bodies, cannot do anything, and we are damn well aware of it? We just slowly rot away." This broke Brian and Lauren.

Long story short, that was what inspired "The Room." I wanted to develop a story that was not only timeless but universal. Who is this person? Male or female? Is this person old, young, middle-aged? I also wanted to throw in the curveball that this person was held hostage in restraints, like in the movie *Saw*. I feel like the story had character, gravity, and the like. Despite the online publication rejecting it, I hope you enjoyed it as much as I enjoyed writing it.

Boxes

Linda was used to clearing her small trinket shop's front entryway of the garbage that would blow in from the street. While she only sold novelties, tchotchkes, and souvenirs, she wanted to keep the store as clean as possible. Her store had only been open for a month, so she tried to keep it in top shape for the summer sales rush. Linda had set up shop in a port town, with her store facing the waterfront. It was a tourist spot, to say the least. She was prepared for the big rush.

Something seemed off today. On this Sunday, Linda stared at a small brown box that someone had gently placed in the store's doorway corner. She picked it up on her way into the store, audibly remarking how light the package was. It seemed nearly empty, perhaps filled with paper goods or jewelry. Linda placed the box on the counter and headed to the back of the store for routine checks.

Much like every other Sunday this month, she spent the day dusting, cleaning the floor, and organizing the shelves. She had plans to open for business today as well; it just wasn't in the cards while she got settled in. She returned to the storefront, taking notice of the small brown box once more. No distinguishing labels marked it, nothing of significance to illustrate where it originated from, apart from a small smiley face logo on the butt end of the box. It may had already been printed on the cardboard or was a company logo. In either case, Linda dismissed it as she pulled open the tape.

She peeled back the adhesive strip and placed the box on the tabletop in confusion. Behind the two folded flaps was one roll of bubble wrap that contained nothing. Absolutely and positively nothing at all.

"What in the world?" Linda exclaimed as she stuffed the wrapping back into the box, then tossed the box into the recycling bin at the store's rear.

As she dusted and cleaned, she kept thinking about that box. Something so trivial shouldn't have bothered her, yet she found her mind constantly wandering back to it. She climbed down from the stool, gave three books that had fallen over a good dusting, and replaced them in their original positions. Her mind drifted back to the box. *Why was an empty container so carefully stashed in her entryway? Who put it here? Was the postal worker running late yesterday and delivered it in the evening?* Linda shook the ideas from her head, focusing on her work.

Several hours later, once she had cleaned the store to her liking, Linda prepared for Monday's first day of summer. She closed the store by first turning off the lights. Next, she placed a cover on the cash register to prevent it from collecting dust. Last, she panned the room as she backpedaled through the door, as always. She nearly stumbled on something that obstructed her path.

"What in the dickens?" Linda vociferated as she gathered her balance on a nearby light post. "I didn't see anyone deliver a box to my store today."

This box was another small brown one but slightly longer than the first box from this morning. She scanned the sparsely populated street. Deciding to leave the box until the morning, she unlocked her door and nudged it inside with her foot. She noticed how unusually light it was, much like the first one. She wondered who was delivering these obscene jokes. Linda was also curious about who was taking the time to send them.

The following morning, cheerful and early as always, Linda arrived at her store. She parked in the customary lot across the street. Linda gave a friendly wave to the owners of the wine and cheese store that neighbored her building. *They are a lovely couple*, she thought. They had greeted her on the morning of her grand opening. A young couple from Massachusetts, if she recalled. They had moved here to start a business venture together. Linda smiled at that as she rounded the entryway to her door.

"Oh, my!" Linda said as she surveyed the street.

There, on the ground at her feet, sat a third small brown box yet not quite as small as its previous corrugated brethren. This one lay maybe a foot, possibly two feet, across the entryway. Much larger than prior shipments, she figured it best to open the front door before heaving a large box inside. When she reached down and clasped the box with her fingers, something odd happened. It scooped right into her hands, as if it weighed nothing. She quickly clutched the box under her arm and dove inside, then locked the door behind her.

"What is this? I don't recall ordering a thing," Linda said as she examined the box.

Again, as before, there were no markings, shipping labels, or product information. The only thing visible was a smiley face character plastered on the top of the box. Only this time, the logo seemed larger. The eyes were more defined. The smile had gained cheek dimples. She compared last night's box to confirm.

"It's clearly not the same thing. Perhaps I got a package by mistake," Linda said, thinking it was a box meant for the next-door wine and cheese couple.

She turned on the store's lights, then exited with the box. The neighboring business door was propped open, indicating they were open. The hours of operation were posted clearly on the door just under the sign, OH CHEESE, WINE NOT? Linda thought it was a creative name for a company, even if it sounded negative. She entered the establishment with her package.

"Linda, hi! How are you?" the wife called out to her.

"Tori, was it?" Linda looked for confirmation before continuing. "I'm great, but I think I got something of yours?" She held out the box.

Tori frowned slightly. "Sorry, sweetie. Not ours. We aren't expecting anything, but I can check with Jeff. Do you mind?" She motioned toward the rear of the shop.

Linda nodded as Tori half-jogged to the back of the store. Linda gently tossed the box back and forth, noticing how light it was even though it was larger.

"Linda, how can I help you? Box of books that needs lifting?" Jeff asked while making a strongman pose.

Linda grinned. She had once used him to move a large bookcase into the store. "No, I just wanted to drop off a package I think was left on the wrong step."

Linda held out the package for Jeff and Tori to see. They eyed each other before refocusing on Linda. It seemed as if Linda was no closer to an answer than she was before.

Jeff pulled a pocketknife from his back pocket. "If it's not ours, and clearly not yours, and it's clearly missing labels, I see no harm in opening it just to figure out what it is, right?"

Jeff's knife sliced gracefully through the brown packing tape. The small threads split easily, like hairs, as he finished his cut. He retracted the blade and secured it in his rear pocket. Jeff carefully lifted the box's left flap, followed by the right.

HIs eyebrow raised, as his upper lip curled. Slowly, he carefully returned the package to Linda. "It's empty. Aside from some packing material, it's empty."

Linda looked into the box again. Jeff was right. Just like the last few boxes, this one too was utterly devoid of a product. She smiled at the happy couple as she closed the box.

"I can take that for you if you'd like." Jeff reached for the box. "Our bin is kinda empty anyway."

Linda passed the box to Jeff. "That's nice of you. Thanks." She hesitated. "I should get back to the store. Hope you guys have a busy Monday."

The couple exchanged a wave with Linda as she exited.

The warm summer air was already getting hotter as Linda rounded the doorway to her store, then she shrieked, "No, no, no, no. This isn't here." Linda pointed at the small brown box resting on her front door.

This box, larger than the last, was at least three feet wide by at least four feet long—bigger than the one she had taken next door. She opened her front door wide and kicked a proverbial game-winning goal with the new box. It was as light as she assumed, allowing the box to sail into the store and crashed into a shelf midway in. She closed the door behind herself and switched her sign to OPEN.

Linda ran the box to the back of the store to dispose of later. She had no need to view the contents. She knew it was from the same sender, clearly noted by the sizable smiling grin on the box and the two beady eyes staring back at her. The teeth of the smile were different, however. She hadn't noticed the grin on the last batch of boxes.

The bell chimed as a customer entered the shop.

Linda figured she'd settle this later with the postman and returned to work.

Near the front, an older man perused some postcards.

"Hey there! How are you this morning?" Linda asked as she hurried back to work in her shop.

"Oh, I'm surviving. By the way, I brought these in for you. I hope that was okay?" The man pointed to a stack of four rather large-size boxes placed by the counter. "They didn't weigh much, so I figured I'd check off my good deed for the day."

Linda shook with fear and anger. Someone was playing a prank on her, and she would get to the bottom of it. She rushed to the phone at the rear of the store and dialed the post office.

The sweet-voiced Jacqui answered her call.

"Hi, Jacqui. It's Linda at In Ornament Objects," Linda said over the phone.

"Hi, Linda. And may I say that is a great store name? Are you the one on First Street? My mother loves your little shop. She's been there twice already! How can I help?"

Linda cleared her throat. "Am I expecting any packages at my business today, by chance?"

Jacqui clacked on some keys on the other end of the line while making audible search noises. "No, I can't see anything for the next few days. Are you expecting a shipment?"

Linda paused, thinking how crazy it would sound if she said someone was dropping off mystery boxes. After all, a handful of other local couriers could be delivering these. "No, just curious is all. Thanks, and take care," she said and set the phone on its cradle.

Linda held the receiver for a moment before letting go. She returned to the front of the store to check if the gentleman needed assistance. Every aisle, every shelf, no one was to be found. *He must have left already*, she thought.

As Linda sorted a small jewelry rack on the front register area, she spotted a familiar brown object in her peripheral vision. Someone was delivering another package to her doorstep. The slight wall of the entryway obscured the delivery person, so she rushed to greet them. A box, labeled and marked, sat at her feet.

The delivery driver approached his vehicle and waved as he drove around the corner.

The package was from her craft dealer, something she had been expecting for days. She gently removed the tape to reveal carefully secured small postcards, adorned with hand-drawn birds, squirrels, and other nature themes. Linda sighed in relief.

She turned to head to the back for the pricing machine, only to find brown boxes now filled several aisles. Some stood six feet tall or more. The smiling face stamped on the side of each box was now human head size, if not larger. Only with more articulation to the face, with ears drawn in, eyebrows, and even a nose. The smile was also slightly gaping, revealing a hint of a tongue as well. Clearly spooked, Linda rushed next door to seek assistance from Jeff and Tori.

Jeff was cutting the cheese in the corner, while Tori poured a wine glass for a potential customer tasting.

"Are you okay? Oh my God!" Tori placed the bottle on the table and rushed to Linda. "What happened?"

Linda trembled, never having been so easily spooked in her life. Now she quivered and was almost in tears because of a box. She swallowed her pride and explained what had been happening since yesterday.

"You mean, someone has been sending you these empty boxes? And the postmaster can't help you with it?" Jeff asked.

Linda sat upright in one of the stools. "No. They couldn't find any shipments. I'm not sure who's doing this, but I'm getting freaked out a bit."

Tori poured a small amount of wine into a glass. "Here, sweetie. This might help take off a bit of the edge to relax. Would you like me to come with you to the shop?"

Linda took a small sip of the wine, then finished off the glass. "No, I think I can manage. I've run the store by myself this far. I'll be fine." She handed the glass to Tori as she stood to leave.

"If you need us, you know where to find us," Tori said.

Linda let the door close behind her, not even looking back. The walk to the store seemed longer than ever. With every step, she knew a box would be waiting to greet her on the doorstep. With each click of her heel on the pavement, she saw the hand-drawn face on the box, heard the tape, and felt the packing inside. Her heart raced as she rounded the corner.

As expected, a large brown box waited for her in the doorway, almost the size of a person and could easily house one if she wasn't so sure it was empty. She quickly flung open the door and tossed the box into the store.

Angrily, Linda stomped on the box, not caring about the contents; she knew it was empty. The cardboard crushed and caved as Linda pushed her foot through each corner, properly flattening the box. Once she expended all her energy and frustration on the box, the only thing left to do was clean up. Linda bent over to gather the box and to dispose of it in the dumpster out back. She did her best to balance it as she fiddled with the door located in the store's rear. In one quick toss and with a smile, Linda hurled the cardboard into the blue dumpster. She stared at it in triumph, lingering for a moment to bask in the victory.

After calming down and collecting herself, Linda returned inside. "No! God, no!" Linda cried out.

An army of boxes had collected inside her store—placed in every aisle, on every surface, and in every corner. Boxes were everywhere. Large brown boxes, complete with a face emblazoned on the side. Only this time, the face was far more detailed. She maneuvered through the crowd of corrugation to find the front of the store. Each turn and twist in the cavern of towering boxes became increasingly confusing. She felt as if she lost her way. The lights dimmed as more boxes appeared in her store. Linda could not breathe anymore; cardboard snuffed out the very air from the room.

Linda used the last lux of light in the cardboard cavern to see the smiling face standing before her—only now it wasn't plastered on the corner of a box. This time, it took the full length of the tallest box, staring down at her, with a detailed grin, menacing beady eyes, and a fully cloaked body. Packing wrap surrounded her body as she fell to the floor, bound and unable to move. As her eyes wandered to her coffered ceiling, a final little brown box smothered the last glint of her lighting.

What's in the Box?

I wrote this in jest, but it became something great. I got the idea when I was wronged by a bookstore. She had someone residing in a spare room of her store, who got too many deliveries, causing boxes to fill their store. Obviously, we know the delivery company was the River Who Shall Not Be Named but will likely sell this book. It went from a quick joke about boxes burying us alive to a story about these supernatural boxes coming to life.

I wanted the idea of a neutral main character. I hate writing a story about a bad person who *gets what they deserve* or about a good person who *does something to get themselves into a pickle*. I wanted to just write something that was very *Tales from the Crypt* feeling, where we explore just a surreal situation without any explanation. There's no rhyme or reason why these boxes are persecuting Linda. She is new to the neighborhood, so obviously she will believe it is a prank. Who would think it is demonic boxes? I know I wouldn't. Then again, I might because that is how my brain works.

I also enjoyed writing the neighboring business. To be honest, I found their characters more enjoyable than anything else. I left myself with the question, "What the heck did they see when they stopped next door after closing up?" Let me even get into how much thought went into the store names. Oh Cheese, Wine Not? cracked me up for no less than ten minutes. In Ornament Objects was also clever to me as well. I don't know why I giggled so much at these, but I get a kick out of stores that have a clever play on words. It also helped create a small business vibe of the neighborhood.

Personally, loved writing this story and almost didn't want to end it. The piling of the boxes as the ominous face enlarged pushed me to realize we had to finish soon. I knew Linda's end was near. Hopefully, you enjoyed the story and the personalities of these wonderful people, as these boxes plagued their lives, as much as I did.

Connecting

Elvira wanted nothing more than to return home from work, cozy up on the couch with her pup Milo, and binge watch a dozen television shows. She finally received her wish when she punched out at five, quickly threw on her nicest Minions pajama set, and snuggled up with Milo and a cup of hot tea.

Fumbling for the remote, she shouted voice commands into it to present her with various guilty pleasure shows, those that she grew up on. "*Friends!*" she exclaimed with glee into the microphone. No response. "Show me *Seinfeld!*" she cried out again, assuming the remote did not recognize her first command.

All at once, she gave up and did things the old-fashioned way. After all, she was the last generation to remember changing the knobs on the television; this was a far cry from those days. She tried to manually navigate the app, thinking it was a voice-command issue.

CONNECTING ...

The message repeatedly blinked on her television in mockery of her desire to watch a program. Over and over, click after click, met with the same issue.

"It must be the TV set," she thought out loud, reaching for her iPhone.

The top of the screen displayed a slash through the bars, and the Wi-Fi signal was unavailable.

"Oh, come on," she yelled to nobody in particular.

Believing it might be a blackout, she donned her slippers and made for the door to check on her neighbor, Norma Jean, whom she had been friends with for some time. She flinched from grabbing the scalding doorknob.

After nursing her wound for a moment, she pulled her sleeves down her palm and pulled open the door, instantly greeted with flames. Fire ripped through the doorway as the heat nearly knocked her off her feet. She peered into the distance beyond the doorway for somewhere to escape.

A large shadowy figure stood before her, with horns crested atop its head. It smiled gracefully as it extended a hand toward Elvira. "Welcome to your eternity, Elvira. We've been expecting you. You remained so distant from everyone throughout your entire life, isolating yourself from everything. This is the Hell you have designed."

Elvira glanced at the television, greeted by the only message she would see for the rest of eternity: CONNECTING …

Connection Issues

I wrote "Connecting" as part of my quick Halloween short-story challenge. I was having issues with my internet and couldn't stream a show I liked, which felt like literal hell because it was the only thing giving me life it seemed. I wrote this story under the pretenses of that very thought; "What if this was Hell, and that's why I can't watch my show?" Obviously, the idea was absurd because it was just my router being stupid, again.

As I wrote, I wanted to create a world that just unfolded before the reader. After you finish, rereading the story makes it so much worse. Poor Elvira is living in Hell, quite literally! She desires to return home and unwind after work, but she is incapable, since nothing works. Could you imagine Hell quite literally being just going to work every day? I don't even mention Elvira's job, so what if it's just the feeling of exhaustion after work, repeatedly?

I posted the story online as I typed, without reading through what I had created. When I reread it, I thought, "Man, that's pretty messed up." A few people responded in agreement. The inspiration for this story was limited to that. A faulty Fire Stick and a defective router.

Ransack Jones (The Ballad)

Ransack Jones was the strongest of any man alive
 Surely, he was the last to think that he would die
Killed himself more than ten dozen men
They surely thought he'd never kill again
Little did they know he'd be back on the prowl
It's not like Ransack to throw in that towel

Ransack, Ransack Jones
They call him that, but nobody knows
Ransack, Ransack Jones
As he breaks and he pillages everybody's homes
Ransack, Ransack Jones
Loyal to no man, until his dying day

Now old Ransack moved to a farm on the hill
To see exactly what was left to kill
He'd fought every man in every corner of the world
Just to be swept off his feet by the tavern keep's little girl
Little Bessy May was no older than twenty
But to Ransack, that was more than plenty
A thin brunette that was more than half his age
Nearly sent his heart to a flutterin' craze

Ransack, Ransack Jones

They call him that, but nobody knows
Ransack, Ransack Jones
Knows how much force to break a man's bones
Ransack, Ransack Jones
A name that's revered all across the plains

Ol' Ransack and Bessy, they moved into that farm
To set up a life together, and boy did Bessy bring out the charm
She hung doilies and daisies and gave it her touch
Poor ol' Ransack even felt it was too much
He hollered and yelled to take it all down
But Bessy had planned how it ought to go down

Ransack, Ransack Jones
They call him that, but nobody knows
Ransack, Ransack Jones
Never met a man who he couldn't beat
Ransack, Ransack Jones
He never saw it coming; he was swept off his feet

Ol' Bessy May left from church that day
She hoped that ol' Ransack would get in her way
She'd planned and processed just what she'd do
Even considered poisoning his stew
But Bessie, she wasn't no fool
She kept things simple, picked up a tool

Ransack, Ransack Jones
He better watch out; Bessie ain't having no more
Ransack, Ransack Jones
He hit her yesterday; today he'll hit her some more
Ransack, Ransack Jones
Resting in a pool of blood on his living room floor

And nobody asked Bessie what she done it for
Because everyone knew they didn't need to know more
As they tossed his body into a shallow grave
Bessie and her Pa celebrated this day

They called him Ransack, Ransack Jones
Relegated now to just a pile of bones
Buried a foot deep under his family home

Why a Ballad Song?

Listen. I don't know exactly what was going through my head. I kept hearing this cowboy jingle, similar to "Rawhide" or something. As I followed the journey, I decided I wanted to write a song about a ruthless cowboy type who met his demise at the hands of a lover. On the surface, it worked in my head. In theory, putting pen to paper—rather, fingers to keys—proved a bit more difficult.

Once I started writing, I thought about my time in the Southwest—the layout, the environment, the overall vibe. Couple that with my playing of a cowboy game called Red Dead Redemption and you had the perfect rootin', tootin', Wild West shootin' jingle to spring from my brain. Okay, maybe it's not perfect, but I enjoyed writing it.

The story started with some scoundrel, Ransack Jones. I didn't really figure out why I gave him that name, so that made for a clever lyric. I took him on a path through robbing, killing, and more, which evolved into him becoming an older man. From there, the goal was for him to find a little lady and to settle down. However, what Ransack didn't realize was the little lady was the daughter of a man who he had wronged.

It's to be assumed that Ransack had pillaged, stolen from, and possibly killed members of Bessie's family or staff. Doing them dirty, Bessie sees fit to exact her revenge by luring him into a false sense of security, then bumps him off. After years of him beating on her and being a turd of a human being, she shoots him, buries him under the floorboards of their family home, and her and her father prosper, reclaiming what was once theirs.

I don't know about you, but I enjoyed it. Who knows? This entry may be relegated to a pile of bones, just like old Ransack Jones.

The Shed

The howling winds tossed the trees against every surface they could touch, creating a tense scraping sound that Ronald couldn't escape all through the night. He did his best to keep his head under a pillow, muffling the world's distractions as best as he could. Eventually, through the cacophony and chaos, Ronald fell asleep.

Ronald awoke the next morning and peered from the window overlooking his backyard to notice that a blue-painted metal shed had appeared overnight. The only likely scenario for Ronald was the gale had blown it in. Confused and curious, Ronald got dressed and stumbled into the yard to inspect the metal construct. It appeared to have landed nearly perfectly center and upright in his yard, adding to his confusion.

A rusted old lock prevented Ronald from viewing the mysterious shed's contents. He had no idea what lay beyond the locked red metallic door. Rust had consumed some of the exterior, making it clear that this wasn't someone's shed that they had failed to properly install. This shed had been around for a while. *They don't make them like this anymore*, Ronald thought.

Ronald fished around his dank basement and found an old pair of bolt cutters. With a spritz of WD-40, they worked good as new. Ronald tested them a handful of times to ensure they opened and closed, then rushed to the backyard's mysterious shed.

Ronald squeezed the handles by placing the sharp edges of the bolt cutters around the widest part of the lock. After several moments of grunting and sweating, he heard an audible *clink* as the lock gave way to the pressure of the cutters. He tossed the bolt cutters behind him and noticed how nicely they planted straight up in the grass. Ronald gave himself a small congratulations for sticking the landing, with a quick fist pump in the air.

The moment of truth came for Ronald. He tightened his robe, ensuring it wouldn't get snagged on anything as he entered the rusty shack. He turned the metal handle clockwise, feeling the tension release from the locking mechanism. The door opened with a massive groan of rust and age. What Ronald saw behind it flabbergasted him.

Inside the door, housed within the rusted old shed, was an exact replica of his backyard. He looked behind himself to confirm the mirror image was identical, down to the bolt cutters planted upright in the grass just behind him. Confused, he entered the shed, stepping into the grass below.

From behind him, the growling of some unknown creature drowned out the chirping birds and the whirring lawnmowers. A large shadow cast against his home. Afraid and unsure, he glanced around to witness a giant, several-story creature towering over him. With lightning-fast reflexes, Ronald dove into the shed before the foot crashed onto his house and yard.

Glowing-eyed creatures leaped from the behemoth's foot. Ronald's heart raced as he slammed the shed door and frantically latched the lock. He scanned the replica of his yard for something to seal it with. A large rusted lock resting on a bench just off to the right of his back door called to him.

Ronald rushed to grab the lock and slapped it around the latch. He heard the banging of the monsters on the other side. The destruction and chaos echoed through the old metal structure. It didn't appear they could get through.

Exhausted and confused, Ronald collected the bolt cutters, tossed them on the workbench, and retired to the upstairs of his house. Ronald kicked off his slightly muddy slippers, walking to the bedroom. He hit the bed, attempting to fall asleep from the excitement. Ronald found himself distracted and unable to sleep as the wind from the impending storm grew louder outside by the minute.

Cleaning out the Shed

This story was part of my *write something you see immediately* challenge from a few years ago. I thought it was a cool idea the second I looked at my very own shed. The idea of some shed landing in the yard from a rough storm seems farfetched but hear me out. It happens.

Okay, maybe not to a fully weighted metal shed, but it happens to pop-up tents and canopies all the time in my neighborhood. It's not uncommon to find a neighbor's gazebo halfway into another's yard from a terrible storm. The idea went on a journey from there into a multidimensional adventure for the main character. He's trapped in an infinite loop, forever diving through that shed that appears in the yard.

Wet

David was a worrier. He regularly gave himself anxiety over every single thing. One day he could be up in arms over the economy. The next, he fretted over the length of his grass. Everything seemed to worry poor David. It should come as no surprise that the most recent rainstorm had David tied up in knots.

David watched the rain coat the earth in puddles as the soil tried to soak up the liquid. Every twenty minutes, David swept the rainwater from his porch to keep it dry. He didn't want the wood to rot, of course. That would devalue his home, which worried him further.

After three days of rainfall, David grew overly concerned. After his morning toast and jam, he noticed a wet spot on his floor. It hadn't been there the day prior, so he figured something had sprung a leak. He wiped down the floor to not warp the linoleum with moisture damage, then headed upstairs to check the bathroom.

Nothing appeared to be overflowing—no sounds of running water, save for the rainfall outside. David returned to the kitchen to assess exactly what was above him.

"Ah, the bedroom closet," he said and darted up the stairs in pursuit of the source of the leak.

David quickly flung open the door and felt the rug. It was dry as a bone. This new house had sold suspiciously cheap, so perhaps some fault in the drainage was the culprit? He pondered as he scoured for leaking water.

After a fruitless investigation, David returned downstairs, plugged in the television—couldn't be too careful about wasted energy, after all—and turned it on. Out the window, he noticed a six- or seven-year-old girl, soaking wet on his porch.

"Heavens, no," he exclaimed, worried the poor girl might catch a cold.

He thrust open the door to find an empty porch, save for several puddles that he would surely need to sweep soon. David slowly closed his door. He knew he had seen someone but must have spotted a television reflection. He quickly retrieved the broom and swept the water from the porch, then relaxed in his easy chair.

David mindlessly flipped through a dozen channels when a drop of water landed on his cheek. Using his index finger, he wiped off the murky-colored brownish water and wiped it on his shirt, then looked up. The little girl, clinging to the ceiling, blinked out of existence just as their gazes met.

David scrambled from his chair and pressed himself against the wall. The dripping sound from inside the kitchen was almost maddening. He composed himself, assuring his own mind that he had seen something on the television and nothing more. David ventured to the kitchen to clean the dripping water once more, where the little girl stood over the puddle as she pointed upward.

Following her finger, David gazed at the waterlogged ceiling. Indeed, something was wrong. A pipe must have burst, leaking this murky-brown water onto his lovely floor. He rushed to the kitchen supply drawer to retrieve a flathead screwdriver and a hammer, then returned to the upstairs closet.

David swung open the closet door and stared at the floor. The carpet was so perfect that he would have to be extra careful not to ruin it. After what felt like hours of gently removing the carpeting, David pulled back the padding to reveal a small hatch door. He reached for a small oval-shaped ring atop the door.

Of all the things David assumed he would find below the access panel, he never expected to see water bubbling from a small copper pipe. David retrieved his plumbing tools and fixed the problem, sorting out the logistics of repairing the ceiling tomorrow.

After closing the hatch with a sense of accomplishment and pride, he turned to face the small girl standing before him. She appeared more visible now. She smiled gently, reaching for David's hand.

"I always told Daddy that pipe leaked when it rained. He never believed me. Thanks for fixing the problem," the girl said and disappeared into the void.

From that day onward, David affirmed to fix any issues he came across, no matter how small, so the spirits may rest easily.

Wringing Out What This Was About

This was another spur-of-the-moment story. Oddly enough, with this one, I won the VA Creative Writing contest for the second year in a row. My first story that had won that award appeared in *Spooky Tales and Scary Things 2*, titled "Roulette." For this tale, I wanted to tell a different type of story. This came from the COVID Lockdown of 2020, where I hosted a simple writing challenge—look around the room and write about the first thing that pops into your head. It was raining, which ended up being my trigger device.

While I wrote, I didn't think; I just typed. I used a neurotic friend as my main character inspiration. I love writing about a tragedy that isn't explained, too. The initial questions I received after the VA Contest were awesome, such as "Did the father kill her?" or "Did she drown?" The fact that the readers dove right to "Did the dad do it?" tells you what kind of person they are, I think.

I leave it open-ended for you. It's your interpretation as to why she died at a young age, assumingly tragic. I will admit, the girl from *The Ring* came into mind when I developed her visuals, which weren't entirely too different. Aside from crawling from the television after seven days, the way they looked was nearly identical in my head.

Personally, I wish I could go into a huge backstory and deeper inspiration behind this one, but it's just not there. I looked out the window, it was raining, and here we are!

Dearest Agatha

My Dearest Agatha,

I hope this letter finds you well. It has been many long nights since I felt your warmest of touches or the kindest of embraces. It feels like a lifetime has passed since we were once schoolmates, bound by an educational prison. Richford High's days felt like they would never end, but they have vanished into the mists of time. Oh, to go back to those days, when I first gazed upon your beauty.

I look upon my reflection in disgust. The lines in my face become more intrusive, as my hair begins to lose the luster it once had. My eyes now a pallid tone, no longer the vivid green they'd once been. I look into the mirror and say, "Rupert, you're still dashing at forty-one!" I feel this gives me the confidence to speak to you once more. I tell myself, "I'm going to do it." Aggie, we will meet again. It has been far too long.

Yours Eternally,

Rupert

My Dearest Agatha,

Oh, how the years had been kind to you! Moving in with me? What a dear you are! We'll be so caught up in each other that the days will fly by. I'm sure you felt awfully buried beneath your responsibilities! It brings me great pleasure to hear of your arrival! Oh, how the crows outside sing praise of you! I shan't waste another moment dillydallying! Before you arrive, I need to tidy up and ensure everything is in order.

Before I bid farewell, know that everything I do, I do it for you.

Longingly Yours,
Rupert

My Dearest Agatha,

It has been many months since your arrival into my abode. I'm not one to critique, but, my dear, we must do something about your hygiene! We have the modern accommodations, so we must find a way to clean you, my dear. Shall we draw the atmosphere into a romantic escapade, light candles, and spend the evening together? I'll draw the bath at once this evening when I return home from work.

Do not fret, my dear. I told you that I would love you no matter what. It was love at first sight, and, after all these years, I'll do anything just to keep you with me. Please understand I did not mean to offend. I'm at a loss of the proper words or means in which to deliver them. Do not mistake my boldness for a lack of kindness. I shall treat you as if you were the royal queen, come to visit this humble peasant.

Until I return, please keep yourself busy. You cannot spend every day peering out of the window. The neighborhood children are growing weary of you.

Yours forever,
Rupert

Dearest Agatha,

I fear someone may be jealous of our eternal love. Deputy Riggins stopped by the house this afternoon but claims no one answered. Several of the county's finest law enforcement visited me at work. We'll discuss this further when I arrive home.

Above all, I was most concerned for you, alone in the house, with no one to protect you! You must have been so scared as they rapped loudly on the door.

I am most relieved you stopped staring out the window! Could you imagine if the officers had spotted you? They'd confront me with a line of questioning I am not quite prepared for. For now, my dear, refrain from resting near the window. It is also doing your skin no favors, allowing it to crisp in the autumn sun.

You are mine, and I shall never lose you. We must be smart about this, my dearest beloved.

Yours in eternity,

Rupert

Dearest Agatha,

I write to you once more to explain that I am not sore at you. I wouldn't dare raise my anger toward such a sweet and pure soul as yours! It is truly my fault, and I shall pay dearly. Deputy Ruggins and his men searched the home and found you. I would color myself shocked; however, I did foresee this. My lawyer explains that once they found your open grave, they followed the trail to my home almost immediately.

A young child had spotted you and recognized you almost immediately as the twentysomething librarian who recently passed of cholera. Time was kind to you, even in death. Your beauty preserved, even if you were mildly decayed. Your eye never lost the beauty it once held, even if it was one.

Well, my dear. I fear this letter is my last. They've advised me to cease speaking to you hence forth, as it is damaging my case against the State. I pray that one day we shall meet in another life. Your husband was not the one for you, and we were destined to be soulmates. May you rest well and wait for me on the other side.

Yours in life and in death,
Rupert

Love Letters to Agatha?

This story came about with an idea I had kicked around for a bit. "What if some guy was absolutely looney toons and dug up his old schoolmate crush to keep her around?" I wanted to tell the story in a series of letters to give the reader the impression that Agatha was very much alive and well. As you read, it comes across as if Rupert was genuinely in love with her. Eventually that devolves into a bit of an obsession—or perhaps a forbidden love. I wanted to drop the reveal early enough—that he had exhumed his one true love's corpse—to give time for another letter from Rupert.

I really enjoy writing timeless stories, too. In "Roulette," I told a story that felt like it took place in Civil War-era America yet was just as current today. With this one, I think with the verbiage and suggestive texts, this seems like it could be an older story. I was once again thinking about the 1700s' to 1800s' America—or even another country altogether. With names like Agatha and Rupert, this could have also happened in the UK.

I wanted to hint that something about Agatha wasn't quite right early on. Spooking the children as she looked out the window was a fun bit of imagery. Could you imagine being a child and seeing a rotting corpse in a loft window? I thought that was a bit of fun to add to the story.

Much like the ballad in this collection, I wanted to write something out of the normal traditional storytelling. I didn't want to

write a story, per se. A series of back-and-forth letters with a be-
trothed was the best thing I could think of, outside of another ballad.

Leafblower

DAY 163 of The Blowening

    I had been doing all I could to log the accounts. I don't know why I even started doing this. At first, it was something fun to joke about with my sister. My personal accounts of the terror from across the street. The Maniacal Maniac of Blowing. The Dastardly Duster. The Blustery Bandit. The names for him could go on. I wrote these down because the world needs to know. The texts between my sister and I were fine, but this became an obsession of mine. The question posted in the mornings: Would there be blowing today?

It was barely daybreak when the familiar whir of the leaf blower began tossing rocks and debris every which way from the silver pickup truck. Frantically and with purpose, he would pass over the ground, the truck, and even blowing the air at times. It was comical, to say the least. I'd watch with concern as he would reach a point where his electric blower would unplug, creating a panic I've never seen in a person before. I've been frustrated when my vacuum disconnected from the wall, but this was a new level of chaos. He would frantically dive for the cord, as if his life depended on it.

Today was like every other as he blasted rocks, leaves, and various other particles every which way from here to Kalamazoo. I left my house to collect the mail and shot him a gentle wave, which he met with a quick stare as he resumed his job. I shrugged as I thumbed through my letters and flyers, ignoring one credit card offer after the next. I gently closed my front door, only slightly drowning out the buzzing outside. My boys wouldn't be home for two more hours, so this was time to myself. I blasted music for the next few hours until Lucas walked through the door.

I logged that my across-the-street neighbor blew through dinner and until nearly two in the morning. He may have been blowing the leaves through the night, but that was when I eventually passed out from exhaustion.

Day 250 of The Blowening

The Blowening, as I had dubbed it so proper, was nonstop. I spoke to my next-door neighbor, Clifford, who was equally infuriated and frustrated with the situation. Cliff assumed The Blower had a disorder or that something just wasn't quite right. As the mother of an autistic child, I 100 percent get that. However, this man didn't seem to exhibit these signs. His expressions told a different story.

Cliff and I would banter about this guy's possible intentions. The consensus was that he was keeping his truck clean to sell it to a dealership. That theory quickly blew away when the end of the year passed. Nobody was that dedicated to vehicle care. My family was lucky if I swung through the local WaWa and vacuumed the interior annually.

While I sat on my stoop, watching the Leaf Blower Man meticulously fan back and forth, as if his life depended on it, I considered grabbing popcorn and a drink. While reading my book and jotting notes of my findings, my son Keith advised me about a fecal situation involving Lucas. What you must understand is that while my life is the furthest from adventurous, my boys ensure my day never remains a bore. I quickly shot up to discover Lucas had suffered a bout of food poisoning and had taken it upon himself to hose down the bathroom wall, so to speak. I only wished it was the upper exit, if you catch my drift.

I lost track of the Blower Man for a while as I bleached the bathroom clean. I nursed my son with the pink liquid to calm his stomach and put him to bed. Once I had everything under control, I peeked out the front window. I don't know what I had missed, but I regretted not being outside to witness how it had transpired.

To my shock and horror, Blower Boy was screaming at his truck. He followed each swear with a kick or a punch toward the truck. The blower lay beside him, smoke gently billowing from the motor exhaust vent area. I only hoped Cliff had grabbed the missing scene. I quickly texted him to ask if he'd seen the activities of the day transpire.

No clue. Dude just started swinging the blower at the truck. Blower smoked a bit, and he resorted to throwing hands.

This was about all I could surmise as well. It seemed this was unwarranted and out of nowhere. Cliff seemed as befuddled as I was, if not more. Exhausted from the bathroom misadventures, I bedded down for the night, shortly after I prepared tomorrow's lunches for the boys. No sooner than I hit the pillow, I passed out.

Day 300 of The Blowening

Cliff and I combined notes on the matter. At first, he thought I was silly to occasionally notate the Blower's accounts. If I had logged every single day, I could publish a book to rival the length of *War and Peace* ten times over. I'd either win a dozen journalism awards or they'd commit me for my meticulous stalking. In either case, I'd be the top of my game.

The sun hadn't even risen when I heard the whir of the blower. About a month and a half ago, he had blown up his last machine, warranting a trip to the hardware store. He had returned with the Gusto 3000, as Cliff and I dubbed it—a gas-powered monstrosity that put out over 300-mph winds and even had a fancy backpack with a kickstand to hold him upright. He had spared no expense, as they say.

He frantically waved the tube over the hood of the pickup, then the wheels. He quickly rushed to the rear of the truck. Cliff shot me a look of concern as Blower Man assaulted the rear bumper with his leather boot. Each swift kick connected with a loud *thud*. I looked toward Cliff again for confirmation that this wasn't a dream.

"No, Daniel San. You must free your mind before you kick the fender. Be the boot. Feel the boot," Cliff said, doing his best Mr. Miyagi impression.

I snorted. Apparently, it was such a violently loud snort that it got the Blower Man's attention. He glared at me for a moment, then his gaze turned once more to worry.

"Thanks, Cliff. Seriously!" I barked at him as I darted into my house and closed my door, which only slightly muffled the sound of the whirring motor.

Day 590 of The Blowening

It has been too fucking long; let's be clear about this. I called the police dozens of times, but they couldn't do anything about him. At least, not yet.

I'm going over there to talk to him 2day

I wanted to reply to tell Cliff to leave the man alone, but part of me wanted to see how this played out. I was afraid for Cliff, so I hid beside my front door, just out of sight, and used my phone to record. Cliff approached the man, who was, right on schedule, blowing away and pushing the same flutter of leaves from left to right, back and forth. I wish I knew what he was thinking.

"*MOOOOOOOOOMMMMM!*" I heard roar out from behind me and winced. I slowly turned around, dreading what abomination my boys had in store for me today.

"Mom!" Keith belted out once more. "Lucas peed in the houseplant again, and I told him not to, but he kept doing it, and I told him to stop, but he laughed and said he was putting out a fire and ... and ... and—"

"Oh, for the love of Betty White. Can you boys just stop for one second? Lucas!"

Lucas stepped in front of the top of the stairway, looking down.

I put my hands on my hips to show I meant business.

"I was wondering if the plant was thirsty," Lucas said innocently.

I quickly rubbed my temples. "The plant needs water, honey. Not your urine."

Lucas looked puzzled. "Urine? But it's out! It's not in me anymore!"

I closed my eyes to momentarily escape this prison of boys before realizing I had a job to do. Cliff needed me. I faced the outside to see Cliff already engaged in a fistfight with Blow Boy. I rushed out immediately to place myself between the two and to calm the situation. Another neighbor stepped outside to intervene.

Cliff grabbed his shirt from the ground, and I escorted him to my porch and sat him down.

"What the absolute fruiting hell were you trying to do out there?" I scolded.

"I was talking to him, trying to get answers, then the prick suddenly blasts me in the face with a whole damn hurricane. I lost my cool."

I felt for him. I don't know what I would have done to the guy if he had turned the blast end toward me at full steam. Probably be in jail, that was for sure.

"You good?" I asked Cliff.

He nodded. "Yeah, just a bit rattled. He didn't even miss a beat, though. He blasted me, then immediately turned back to the truck."

"Odd duck, that one."

"*Odd duck?* That guy is *cuckoo for Cocoa Puffs* at a minimum. Just look at him!"

I refocused on the truck. Blower Man was frantically blasting away at the tires, mirrors, undercarriage, and anything else he could reach. He would kick and punch the truck, the air, and himself from time to time, before he resumed blowing the pickup.

"I don't think there's much we can do," I said.

Cliff shrugged and approached his front door. I gave up and did the same. I had a houseplant to drain, after all.

Day 790 of The Blowening

Two years. Two years of his incessant blowing. I never thought it would stop. I figured this would be my life. I couldn't uproot my children from their schools. I wouldn't find a new home, not in this economy, at least. This was my life, and I must learn to like it or lump it, as they say.

This morning, however, I had just about had it. I was at my wit's end. For that matter, wit ended ages ago. I don't know where the heck I was at this point. Just after sunrise—the sky's orange hue cast an eerie haze on everything—sure as the oven was hot, he was blowing away but looked defeated. I felt for him, honestly. Day in and out, he would blast the truck, the ground, and any debris that came within fifty feet of this neighborhood.

He whipped the air from left to right, frantically blasting debris far and wide. An elderly neighbor approached him to kindly ask him to stop blowing at six in the morning. Without hesitation, he turned the air to her, nearly knocking her on the ground with his vortex maker.

That was the last straw. Cliff stormed through his door, dressed in his work uniform. He pocketed his office lanyard and ID Badge. I knew it was on, like peanut butter on toast.

"Cliff! No," I yelled as he threw the first punch.

I couldn't grab my deadbolt fast enough. My fingers fumbled with the tumbler a dozen times as I frantically flung open the door. When I stepped outside, Cliff had already thrown the blower across the parking lot and pinned the man to the ground.

"Cliff! What the hell?" I cried out, my emotions ranging from exasperation to confusion.

This wasn't the guy I knew. This wasn't who I had attended *Hamilton* with several years back. This wasn't the cultured, museum-hopping, loveable idiot I had come to love as a neighbor. This was someone who was at his wits end with someone else.

Before long, police sirens screamed around the corner. Flashing blue and red lights filled the cul-de-sac as they pushed through the neighborhood. Officers piled out their vehicles by the numbers, demanding that Cliff stop. They subdued my friend, slapping cuffs on him. He thankfully complied.

Blower Boy, on the other hand, had different plans. He lunged for an officer, futilely swiping at the patrolman's back, before another officer restrained Blower Boy. I did my best to remain calm. Unfortunately, I was shrieking frantically and creating my own level of ruckus. An officer escorted me across the street as they placed Cliff and Leaf Man into separate squad cars.

"Would you like to give a statement, ma'am?" Officer Nice asked me. That was his name. I'm not being flippant. I thought it was great. He just needed his partner, Officer Friendly, and we would have been in business here.

"I can. Right now?"

He squeezed my shoulder with his right hand. "You can come to the station when you're ready, or I can wait a few moments for you to compose yourself."

I was perplexed as to what he meant, then realized I was still wearing my SpongeBob pajamas and hadn't yet prepared the children for school. The morning had been so intense that everything was on pause.

"Can I come to the station later? I have to get myself and the kids together."

Officer Nice smiled. "I can do that. Let me get your name and information, and I'll see you, say, noon?"

I smiled and obliged, then returned to the house to gather myself. The kiddos were already putting themselves together. Bless their hearts, they tried. Keith wore chainmail from the last time we had dined at Medieval Times. And Lucas wore, well, he had socks on, at least. I quickly sorted them out and placed them on the school bus.

Keith and Lucas sat in their seats and waved goodbye. The driver smiled as she closed the door and pulled off. The bus rounded the corner and disappeared from my view before I rallied for an eventful afternoon. I noticed a spatter of blood near the toppled leaf blower. A monument to a trying time, that was for certain. As I turned away, something caught my eye near the rear tire of the truck. I did a double take to see what it was.

A neighbor's cat? An oversized rat? No, it didn't look like anything I knew. It was too agile to be a dog as it disappeared behind the tire. I crept toward the truck, then nearly stumbled over the leaf blower when the creature reappeared. At first, it looked like a mangy cat. Its hair was patchy in some places yet missing in other areas. A gray withered body held the tire with razor-sharp talons attached to bony appendages. The face. I'll never forget the face. It had the wildest, most sinister grin I'd ever seen in my life.

Instinctively, I grabbed the leaf blower and revved it up, hearing the familiar droning noise I had come to despise. I blasted the critter with all ten million RPMs of windy death. The creature lost its grip on the tire and disappeared. I started to shut down the machine, but another, if not the same one, reappeared on the truck bed. I blasted that one with another gust of fury. When the next one materialized, I studied it before blasting it to Kingdom Come. This looked like something from a Bugs Bunny cartoon. It was a flipping gremlin.

If not for my sister visiting, I don't think I would have had the chance to write this down, to visit Officer Nice, or to vouch for Cliff and, unbeknownst to me, for Blower Man. I briefed Cliff on the way home about my experience. We vowed to help Larry the Blower Man combat the creatures for as long as we could. Cliff and I splurged on the best leaf blowers that we could afford to help Larry when we could.

Larry battled the gremlins until his heart gave out, several years later. Larry was not a nuisance at all, rather, a hero to the neighborhood. Cliff and I promised to take the burden unto ourselves for as long as possible.

I will no longer log my accounts in the journal, as it would become redundant. I lack the time to write as well. Cliff has yet to see a gremlin, but he takes my word for it. I give him direction, and he blasts.

Day 4,813 of Blowing Away Gremlins

It has been several years. Larry's nephew finally stopped paying for his home and had his truck towed. It got quiet immediately after, and I haven't seen another cryptid on my stoop since. My arms were exhausted, and I hadn't slept right in ages. Neither Cliff nor I knew what the hell we had just experienced, but we'll never be the same after that. That is for dang sure.

Did This Story Blow or What?

This was a unique story, for sure, but I can't take credit for the inspiration. My friend Hey's neighbor—gremlins aside—would leaf-blow his truck for hours. Day in and out, he'd whip wind across the parking lot. It didn't matter what season, weather, or condition. He would blow in torrential downpours. He would blast in a giant windstorm. Nothing deterred this man.

This isn't even the half of it. The police *have* been involved. The neighbor *has* fought folks over it. He *does* mutter to himself, screams obscenities, and kicks the vehicles as he blasts the truck. Honestly, aside from saying, "What if I added gremlins to this," the story is almost frame-for-frame with the real-life experiences.

The kids! The two sons were my favorite part to write. When they were little, in real life, a day didn't go by where Hey wasn't telling us her experiences and stories with these two handfuls. They're both awesome kids, but, man, they did some things that I think warranted sharing. Hey constantly posted about requiring bleach and cleaner due to a poop catastrophe or some other bodily function gone awry.

I wanted to ensure to include these guys, because they are critical to the grounding of the story. Yes, their situations seem over the top, and they only exist to provide comedic relief, but that's basically what they do daily anyway. They're great kids, but in their younger days, they were an absolute handful.

The neighbor? That was basically a mix of myself and Hey's neighbor who lived on the ground floor during this tremendous ordeal. I was the absurd half, and Jay the real neighbor was the other half, forming Clifford, the wonderful neighbor with a heart of gold. We've both offered our hand to deal with this guy as much as possible, with no viable solution.

And Blower Man? Were you wondering what happened to this guy? Well, he's still very much alive and well, with a beautiful new blower, blasting away at the truck as always. He has been nonstop. Rain, snow, sleet, or hail, he'll blow in any condition, at any time. The police have been called numerous times, but nothing has deterred him yet. Please wish Hey the best in her endeavors as she slogs through, day after day, of the familiar droning buzz of the leaf blower motor.

Warning: No Label

I'd like to address the fact that I'm perfectly aware of how we got here. The downfall of humanity and the utter demise of intelligence. To reflect on the ways in which we, as a society, gave up being civil in favor of the current bandwagon trend. I've gone along for the ride, not believing we could creep further into the madness we've invoked. Yet here I was, knee-deep in one of these many poor decisions in our modern life.

I must walk you back several years for you to grasp this complexity. It all started five years ago, during the presidential campaigning, when my wife became enamored with a candidate, enjoying his every word. I was the least political. Dinner conversations became heated and nothing but argumentative.

"You don't understand, James! He'll bring this country back together," Alisson said while twirling her pasta on her fork.

I studied my uneaten food, disgusted by the possibility of the oncoming fight, and said nothing.

"See? That's the problem. You've got no balls, Jim. Just like your mother said, you're a spineless worm who will just go with the flow."

I listened as she barked at me. I didn't have the fortitude to stand up for myself, never have. I let my boss walk all over me at work. Coworkers would take advantage of me. It was just my nature. Alisson was right.

"Oh, just sit there, quiet? Fine. I didn't want to talk anyway," she scoffed as she increased the television's volume.

I remember the broadcast as if it played in front of me now—the day when President Herbert kicked it up a notch. He was my least-favorite candidate, to be frank. At the time, he was trailing in the polls and needed a swift kick to bring him ahead. We were weeks from Election Day, finding ourselves rooting for Candidate Lindsay instead. He had some solid ideals and seemed like a man of the people, until he wasn't.

Herbert spoke out of turn during the debate. It wasn't uncommon for him, but he interjected with the boldest statement uttered on live television. "I'm sick of this country. I'm so tired of it being weak and unable to defend itself. I want to add to my plan—the De-pussification of America Plan. It's a great plan."

Herbert paused for dramatic effect. His words hung in the air and floored the timekeepers, mediators, and most of the viewing audience, then he continued his deluge of insults toward the country's weaknesses. "I propose we do something about it. You know, I was thinking about warning labels the other day. Fun things, great things. Why do we have them? They're dumbing us down and coddling us, thinking we're too stupid to understand that we shouldn't eat rat poison? It needs to be plastered on the box?"

The moderator, a prominent news anchor, tried to step in. "If you could please—"

"That's the problem with this country. I start to talk about the truth, and some pansy news reporter wants to stifle it. Censorship, that's what this is. I thought we were a country built upon the backs of freedom. Where is that? Where is our freedom?"

The crowd erupted in an unusual cheer before he proposed dozens of wacky ideas to improve this country. Some of them sounded just credible enough to make sense.

"You believe this guy?" I asked Alisson, who gazed at the glowing screen.

"He's right. Get this shit out of here. Why do we need to be censored?" she blurted out.

I stared, barely knowing my own wife. We ate dinner and did not speak to each other for the rest of the night.

As the weeks passed, I noticed a change in Alisson. She wore shirts that read DE-PUSSIFY AMERICA! and hung on every word. It was only inevitable that Herbert won the Office of the Presidency by a landslide. I couldn't believe where this was going. Here was a man with a tarnished history, full of prostitutes and drug use, running our country.

The first few months of his tenure were inconsequential. He enacted a bill to boost the Veterans Affairs' funding and structure, which gained a lot of momentum from his constituents. The senate backed his bill in the most one-sided voting I'd ever seen, like this guy was a god or something—the sway he had over people. I wasn't opposed to it, though. The veterans deserve so much more than we give them.

By the end of the first year, we finally saw the De-pussification Policy, as it was affectionally known around the streets. With a resounding *yes* from both the Senate and Congress, it became what we will historically know as the worst decision that toppled the world. They enacted the America Strong Bill on March 10, and things rapidly moved from there. The initial focus was on warning labels. As President Herbert stated in his address to the people, "We simply don't need these things. They're making us soft, and our enemies view us as weak."

The worst-case scenario happened, an undoing of massive proportions. Several centuries of civilized life unfolded before my eyes. The worst part was the news reports. Night after night, overdoses or burns filled the feed. We had no indications that we shouldn't ingest hot coffee. It was like people had forgotten overnight. One such case had a guest speak on *The Oprah Winfrey Show* about her esophageal scarring. The woman omitted the fact that we could have spared her with a simple warning.

I regarded Alisson with a different lens from there on out. She became a different person, one whom I didn't recognize anymore. She stayed out late at rallies and protests. She had been pushing for the removal of what they perceived as a warning label, therefore, making us *soft*. I watched the reports in horror of our troops returning from the front line with injuries from explosives. Our men and women were sacrificing their lives in ways that didn't better anything. They immediately threw out a few warnings, such as *Face Toward Enemy*, but nobody knew which way a claymore should face. It resulted in a lot of tragedy.

We had a few more awkward dinners past that. I would come home from work, narrowly surviving the drive after the removal of yield signs a week prior. Alisson was decked out in full regalia of merchandise, promoting the country's current state of affairs. I could barely look at her anymore.

"You're not eating?" she asked and slurped her soup with delight.

I hesitated but let my emotions get the better of me. "How can I? Look at everything outside. Look at yourself! Have you seen who you've become?"

Alisson aggressively set down the bowl. "Who *I've* become? I grew balls; that's who I became. How about *you*?"

I noticed Alisson's T-shirt displayed the phrase AMERICA HAS BALLS, accentuated with a large scrotum hanging between the red-white-and-blue lettering of the two *Ls*. It looked like a five-year-old had drawn it. How was I supposed to argue with someone who was wearing nuts, while also being completely nuts?

"You've changed, that's all. This whole thing is getting out of hand," I said and stood.

"*I*? *Me*? Are you kidding me right now, Jim?" She slapped her bowl across the table and stormed out.

I chose not to follow. I couldn't follow her where she was going, and that was the reality of the matter. Each passing day in this hell we were building for ourselves grew worse.

Three years have passed since the adoption of the policies that threw our country into chaos. Prior to the downfall, America intimidated the major powers of the world. Russia, followed by Australia and Great Britain, were the first to adopt a similar policy. Not to be outdone, Germany, Canada, and, eventually, the rest of the world followed suit. Year three was a genuine test of fortitude—physically and mentally. For someone like me, emotionally as well.

Alisson moved back in with her parents, leaving me alone in the apartment. I had no further contact with her after that point. Through the grapevine, I heard that a lawnmower had injured her father, who ignored the warnings to shut off the engine and to block the blade before repairing. I never learned the severity of his injury. I felt like a slice of my life was missing, but I sure as hell didn't miss seeing the giant nut sacks adorning the walls and closet.

Another year passed, and the world became more chaotic. In my opinion, this was more than plenty to impeach the elected buffoon. I hadn't voted that year, but I considered voting this time. I didn't, ultimately chickening out before driving to the polling house. It ended up being a decision I would regret. Like a nightmare on repeat, the majority elected President Herbert again. Much like the last round of votes, this was a landslide victory. Herbert seemed smug and pleased with himself.

The new term dove deeper into implementing the changes than ever before. The Removal Committee, as they had dubbed themselves, eliminated roadway signs, railway warnings, and other important traffic-control symbols. A group of appointed advisers, each stupider than the last, voted on what seemed like an item that would make our country look weak. Most were so out of touch with reality that I was shocked it took us this long to fall this far.

The world pulled itself apart. The longer I watched the local news, the more I noticed the decline in the interviewees' intelligence. I headed to the grocery store for some much-needed sustenance. The streets were pandemonium. Chaos filled each intersection, as the removal of traffic lights had prompted an additional problem.

I recalled the senator's press conference regarding their dismissal: *"Many foreign countries understand courtesy and the right of way, never having a collision. I vote we adopt this new way, as I know when to slow down or when to stop my car."* A resounding number of harrumphs and small talk had erupted in the auditorium. Astonishingly enough, the vote had been nearly 100 percent in favor of the removal of the lights. I have watched videos of insane traffic patterns in India and in other countries, but I never expected to drive in one of those intersections in my hometown. Americans were not as courteous and skilled, however. As one could imagine, the worst-case scenario unfolded in the following weeks.

I needed to get out of this house. Something about what was nearly marathoning hourly on the television boiled my blood. I needed a few necessities, so I figured the nearby grocery store would be a good bet. I just needed to clear my head. I grabbed my wallet and keys, then strode to the line of parked cars along my road. We had recently omitted the fire lanes and the No Parking signs, which was an open invitation to every asshole SUV owner to double park alongside the road. I was old-fashioned and still parked in the lot across the street.

Luckily for me, people still managed to park within the remnants of the lines. That was one thing that didn't change abruptly. I pulled out and navigated to the highway, bound for sustenance. I sped onward, pushing sixty into the fray of traffic. Trucks and sedans whizzed past as I tried to accelerate. I couldn't make heads or tails of the traffic flow, dodging an oncoming vehicle in my lane. It had gotten worse since they removed the direction signs. Nobody knew what was a one way, a no entry, and so on.

I heard a familiar sound behind me. The red and blue lights flashed from behind me as I steered toward the shoulder. Instinctively, I reached for my license and registration.

"What's the trouble, Officer?" I asked, seemingly confused.

The officer rested his hand on the windowsill. "Do you know how fast you were going back there?"

I checked my speedometer, hoping it would contain the answer. I tried for the life of me to recall how fast I was going. "Seventy?"

"Seventy-five," the officer replied as he adjusted his sunglasses.

I produced my credentials. "Here's my info. Sorry, I wasn't sure how fast to go."

"Hell, I'm with you on that, buddy. Old habits die hard. Been on the force for over twenty years, and this is the first time I'll let a blatant speeder go, due to lack of signage. Old dogs and new tricks, ya know?"

I withdrew my papers and placed them in the center console for safekeeping. "Well, okay then?"

"Drive safe, sir. It's crazy out there." The officer tapped my car's roof and returned to his patrol vehicle.

I sat in the car for a moment, trying to figure out what had just happened. I'd been ticketed many times when I was younger and not once had they ever let me just leave. I started the engine and resumed my journey to the grocery store.

I narrowly dodged a two-car collision that escalated into a five-car pileup on the freeway to Kroger. I just wanted to reach my destination and get home safely before something terrible befell me. I knew I would have to take the back roads home, too. Traffic was a nightmare, even without accidents. The parking lot resembled a demolition derby, as some considered the parking slots too contrite and deemed them *hand-holding* per our local governor. Our county official determined we should *just know* where the handicapped should park and removed the signs accordingly. The whole situation spiraled out of control, border lining silly, if you ask me.

The grocery store doors were a welcomed sight after narrowly escaping death three times. The landscape had shifted drastically in the past half-decade. The air smelled of rotting meat and fruit. Expired goods littered the aisleways. We had abolished expiry dates last October, making it nearly impossible to know when meat was bad, until it was obvious. I remember last year's Salmonella outbreak nearly wiped out the world's population, one chicken breast at a time.

I trekked through the store toward the cereal aisle for a box of Lucky Charms. Cereal was a safe bet, but you had to eat it dry. The dairy aisle was so rancid with spoiled milk that it was hard to determine what was edible. When I reached the checkout counter, I noticed they had removed the buffers between customers' items.

"They get rid of the little sticks?" I asked the cashier as she scanned my cereal.

"I'm not stupid. I know what stuff is yours." She waved my box of cereal around. "See? Cereal. If someone put grapes behind you, I know that's their grapes."

I said nothing more. Another byproduct of this happy shift in climate was the attitude problem everyone had caught. People were shorter-tempered and easily agitated. Her snarky comment made me nearly snap back, but I kept my cool. It wasn't worth it. I set the ten-dollar bill on the counter and told her to keep the six-cents change.

I sauntered to the car as I reflected about how cereal used to be five dollars when I was a kid. My mother would always say, *"Jimmy, we're not made of money,"* before grabbing the store brand for a dollar less.

I tossed the box into the passenger seat, dialed my radio to a good station, then used the back roads to drive home—my favorite mode of travel on certain days. They always had little-to-no traffic and weren't prone to the same drama and chaos of the highways and interstates. It was my little oasis in the calamity of the outdoors. I often stopped by the little park near the lake to just behold the scenery. The stupidity of man had somehow left the outdoor paradise untouched. I continued that tradition, pulling off the paved path and onto the dirt road. It was always bumpy and likely took a toll on my shocks, but the payoff was worth it.

I reached the large old-world stone bridge that connected my paradise to the rest of the world—something from the original settlers, more than likely. I'd only driven over it a handful of times in the past few months, but it seemed more than sturdy to handle my ride. I crossed with ease while the radio blared Lynyrd Skynyrd. I parked at the little bench I frequented and felt the soft breeze on my face as I reached for my cereal. The sky was overcast, and it could rain at any minute. Truthfully, I would welcome the rain, as it would only add to this beauty of the world.

I sat on the table, feet planted on the bench, facing the water. The waves lapped the rocks on the shore as the breeze increased slightly. I didn't care as I stuffed my face with marshmallows and dry cereal while browsing my phone.

WOMAN KILLED IN DEADLY ELEVATOR INCIDENT the headline read. I figured I had nothing else but to explore such a jarring topic from the local news post. I continued to read it. *Local woman Alisson Moxley found dead after a tragic elevator malfunction caused her to plummet forty stories down the shaft.*

I paused and reread the opening line. Alisson Moxley. My ex. She had reverted to her maiden name pretty quickly, too. I skimmed the rest of the article, my mind not fully grasping the words as my gaze went from line to line. They had removed broken elevator signs just last month, and Alisson had failed to recognize that the cables were weakened. This was an *operator error*, the article went on to say.

"Jesus Christ," I said and spit out marshmallows and cereal bits onto the table.

No one was near me to hear my shock, save for a squirrel or two. I took another handful of cereal, chomping loudly with each bite. I wanted to feel sad. I wanted to be angry for her, but this was the world she had chosen to build. The sissy ways were gone, as she would boast. Who knew the importance of a broken elevator warning? As I scrolled through my social media news feed, raindrops fell on my phone screen and into my cereal box.

Great.

The rain turned into a downpour, and I muttered some things about how I had forgotten my umbrella. I was fine with riding out a drizzle, but the monsoon that erupted was too much for me to handle. I retreated into my car, evading the storm as best as I could. A torrent of water burst from the sky and doused the ground. I could barely see five feet in front of the windshield. I opted to take myself home and to get out of these wet clothes.

I started the car and flicked the windshield wiper level to High, the wipers kicking into gear and wicking away the water as quickly as possible. It gave me a bit more visibility, which was just enough to get moving. The ground was muddying, and I didn't want to get stuck out here. I shifted into Drive and edged toward the main roads.

I rounded several tree-filled corners, many of which had downed branches and limbs littering the road. I did my best to evade them as I veered to the bridge. I slowly crossed, staying careful not to steer to the sides and topple over. The sides weren't that high as it were, so my SUV would have gone over without a fight.

I reached the middle of the bridge, but my car became lodged in something. A downed tree limb, perhaps? I lowered my window to see if I could catch a glimpse of it, the rain flooding the driver's seat.

I realized what it was. It was no tree branch. It was no log. I wasn't caught in a loose puddle of mud. I found myself face-to-face with a matter of human engineering. The bridge that my ancestors had painstakingly crafted hundreds of years ago had now become so eroded with decay and from lack of maintenance that it now crumbled under the weight of my car.

I considered escaping my fate. I plotted how to get out safely. It was futile as the center of the bridge collapsed, and my vehicle plunged into the freezing waters, fifty feet below. As the water approached fast, I only had a single thought.

They could have at least kept the bridge weight limit signage in place.

Caution: May Contain Information

This really cool idea unfortunately wasn't my own. I was attending a horror festival, Monster-Mania, and a nice woman named Kim struck up conversation with me. We discussed a bunch of things, such as the length of the lines, how tired we were, and the building's hot temperature. Eventually, it came up in conversation that I was a writer. This is where it all unfolded.

Kim said she would love to read a story about an idea she had and described a world without warning labels. I was immediately interested but told her that I couldn't promise anything and gave her my card. We chatted about some of the possible absurd things of the story. Between coffee cups without the Caution: Hot! warning or the Do Not Eat! labels on certain things, we were off to a fantastic start.

From there, I brainstormed some ideas and wondered how far I could take the omissions, from road signs to emergency beacons. The story delved deeper into Stupidsville quickly. I dug the idea. The only problem was that I was nose-deep into writing *Chemical Burns* with author Tim Baldwin, which took all my attention.

Fast forward to the next year, and I finally churned it out. I was delighted with myself, to be honest. Incorporating a recent presidency as the backbone of inspiration, I created a world that tried to out-do itself in machoism. America does a thing, the UK does something in reply, and Russia responds. Sounds pretty close to home, right? Exactly.

I could pepper so much realism into it because of the COVID-19 pandemic, our interesting four years of cults and fascism, and more. I tossed all that into the narrative while we followed this poor protagonist on a journey full of red flags—if they were allowed in this world, that is.

So, once again, thanks for the fun idea, Kim. I hope it turned out as you had hoped. Maybe we'll run into each other at FrightReads Book Festival or at Monster-Mania, and we can talk about another great idea!

Moonroof

The weather was pleasant, so I agreed to let my wife turn off the car. I had elected to stay outside while she completed errands. The parking lot, to my surprise, was rather empty for a Saturday afternoon, but that could be expected of the good weather. Most families were likely at the beach, were camping, or having some amusement park adventure. Contrarily, I was here, waiting in an SUV, while the midday sun bore down as a gentle gust of cool air counteracted the heat.

One of the more unique features of this car was the moonroof. I had always wanted one but never felt the need. I preferred air conditioning to blow on me year-round. However, there was something to be said about a temporary luxury. I requested that to remain open for the duration of her shopping. I planned to recline the chair and observe the clouds, the nearby maple tree, and any other outside happenings. My wife obliged before killing the engine.

A family behind me approached the store while debating where to eat lunch or some other trivial topic. I, however, relaxed in the near silence of the afternoon. The occasional passing vehicle broke the peaceful chirping of the birds, but I didn't mind. I checked my social media, watching two or three videos, before resuming my rest.

I gazed at the blue sky, tinted only slightly by my sunglasses, as the sun ever-so-gently slid behind a large cloud, which did wonders for the weather. I was reflecting on my life, on my day, and was truly taking in what it meant to be on this planet when something obstructed my view. A dark object flashed past my vision, momentarily darkening the SUV. I assumed it could be a jetliner, as we weren't far from the airport. I sat up a bit for a better view and couldn't see a plane preparing to land. Perhaps someone had walked too close to the SUV and had managed to blot out the light on one side?

I shifted my weight, finding my solace once more. I shut my eyes, lulled by the gentle chirping of the nearby robin nest. I had nearly nodded off when the flash of darkness passed over again. Sitting upright, I scanned all directions. No plane in the sky. The cloud wouldn't have created that much darkness so quickly. Soon, I spotted it across several parking spaces, high atop a parking light. I couldn't quite discern what it was.

I adjusted myself better to glimpse the creature. My first assumption was an eagle or some larger bird of prey. They were common around here, as the local creek provided a plentiful supply of fish. I was no bird expert, but I can assure you that this was nothing I'd ever seen before—prehistoric, almost mythical. Quite Eldridge, to be frank. The plume atop its head, to the jagged spiked tail feathers, seemed alien to me. I slouched into the seat to keep an eye on it while also not provoking it.

It seemed that in my haste to hide, I alerted it to my presence. The creature swooped and did a close pass over the moonroof before ascending toward another light. I quickly assessed my surroundings to check if any passersby had noticed what I'd seen. The lot was vacant, save for a few cars and stray carts, so I did the most logical thing; I texted my wife.

I must have sounded insane, pleading for her to hurry up. I could have just as easily joined her, but I wasn't sure what the hell this thing was or what it was capable of. The car was more than enough protection and deterrent to keep the creature at bay. I frantically refreshed my messages, hoping she would agree to come out to at least look at the car, then assess what to do. I needed guidance from an outside view, as the only things I was finding myself capable of were terror and fear.

Minutes passed, which felt like days. I awaited a response. I glanced at the shop, which seemed miles away, although we were six spaces from the road separated the building from the parking lot. If I could just bide my time until the bird flew to the farthest post, I could easily make a break for it. I looked through the open moonroof to get a better view of the beast. Before I could peer around to see, the damned thing thrust its beak into the moonroof.

I panickily whirled around to my car door and opened it slightly, then quickly pulled the seatbelt toward the bird. In my haste, I combated the safety mechanism that prevented quick yanks. After frantically fighting for a few tugs, I finally gained enough slack to wrap the seatbelt around the beak of the poor demonic beast. As the beak thrust deep into the console, I twisted and tightened. I took one extra step; I buckled the belt.

As the bird fought to break free, I knew my moment had come. I quickly kneed open the door and left it ajar as I hightailed it for the shop. I didn't look back. I didn't care to see its enormous wingspan looming behind me as I sprinted. I dashed toward the automatic doors in the hopes they'd cooperate with my panic. They slid open with a generously polite *ding* as I scuffed across the vestibule carpeting.

Without a moment to waste, I pushed the doors shut, fighting the automatic system along the way. I latched the lock and peered into the parking lot. The bird was free of its consumer safety-rated prison. I rushed into the store to alert the clerk. I must have looked like a madman.

The young man, easily a high-schooler or freshly graduated, stared at me with his pimple-ridden face, as if I was speaking a foreign language.

"The bird! You didn't see the bird?" I screamed, realizing I was now escalating to the level of a raving lunatic.

"Mister, calm down. What bird? I didn't see no bird out there—or whatever you're talking about," the kid started. "Is there someone in this store you're looking for?"

I took a moment to catch my breath. I slicked my hair to the side and composed myself while fixing my shirt. "My wife. She's in here somewhere. Can you page her?"

The young man raised an eyebrow.

I spied his nametag before he turned to the phones. "Andrew," I muttered.

As Andrew made the page, I periodically eyed the parking lot. No shadow. No bird. As if I'd imagined it. I was sure that was it—my imagination. I had likely daydreamed an encounter with a typical pigeon, and my brain had worked overtime, and voilà—death bird from Hell. Seems logical. My wife always told me that my brain ran a mile a minute and was more inventive than mankind over the past sixty years.

Something grasped my shoulder. I jumped backward, nearly toppling my wife.

"What? What's wrong that you have to have me paged?" she asked.

"I... uh... couldn't find you in the store, and you didn't answer your phone. I figured this would do the trick."

It must have been a good enough cover because she bought it. She checked her phone, noticing the three missed calls from me, as well as a text message or two. She didn't bother to read the messages, rather she returned her phone to her purse.

"Are you ready to check out?" Andrew asked.

"I suppose so," my wife said begrudgingly.

She shot me a look as Andrew scanned the items. I guess I had cut her shopping expedition short today. All's well that ends well, I suppose. I pulled out my card to pay the ticket, as it felt like the most appropriate gesture, given how I had prematurely ended her adventure.

"Thank you and be sure to take the survey at the bottom of the receipt. You get entered into a drawing for a fifty-dollar gift card," Andrew exclaimed as he handed me the receipt, then waved us off as he moved to the next customer.

Walking alongside my wife, I watched her push a shopping cart filled with the day's treasures. I was so at ease that I nearly forgot about the bird. Midway between the store and the parking lot, standing in the center of the road, I looked around. My gaze darted from each end of the building, up and down and all around. No sign of the Hell bird anywhere.

"What are you looking for?"

"Nothing. Just thought I heard an airplane or something," I said, as poor of an excuse as I could muster.

She shrugged me off and continued toward the car. No ominous shadows. No screech. Nothing. She popped the trunk as I loaded the purchases into the back. As always, she pushed the cart to the corral to get in her steps. I never understood the hype over fitness watches, but if she was being heathy, I guess they were not too bad. The rest of the doors unlocked, and I grabbed for the passenger door. I pulled it open only to be met with absolute horror.

Before I could react to the reality of the situation, I could already hear the commotion from the other side of the car.

"What the hell did you do out here?" my wife shrieked. "The car is wrecked!"

I climbed inside a bit to get a better look. She was right. The entire center console was torn to shreds. The moonroof was shattered and scratched. The roof looked like it had been in an absolute warzone during a hailstorm. I peered around one more hopeless time, hoping to explain the horrors I had just endured. It wasn't a dream. It wasn't a figment of my imagination.

I spent the twenty-minute car ride home trying to figure out a great explanation. Maybe I just tell her that I had left the moonroof open, and a dog had gotten in? Every idea I concocted seemed more farfetched and asinine the deeper I dug. I finally decided the proper thing to do was to tell the truth. I mustered the fortitude to explain to my wife that a giant prehistoric bird creature had stalked me and had tried to eat me.

"Honey, I—"

"What is that?" she interrupted as she slowed the vehicle.

Ahead was an overturned pickup truck. The tires looked like something had chewed them off. As I began to tell her the terrifying tale I had found myself in, a shadow passed over the car. I glanced through the demolished moonroof and saw my alibi gliding down toward the vehicle. I guess I wouldn't have to explain my way out of this one after all.

What's The Word on the Bird?

I came up with it, ironically, while relaxing in my wife's car, waiting for her to shop. The weather was beautiful for the time of year—a crisp sixty-five degrees—and the windows were down, while the moonroof was open. My kind of weather, as fall and spring (the good parts of them) are the best weather around. I'd die on that hill.

As I sat in the car, I noticed a large shadow pass overhead. I spotted the biggest damn seagull I'd ever seen, sitting on a light post across from the hood of the car. As it turned out, an aircraft had passed over the sun, blocking it and casting a shadow nearly perfectly timed to the bird landing on the pole. One in a million chance, as it were.

I grabbed my phone and jotted down my idea. *Some kind of evil bird tries to kill me while waiting for my wife to finish shopping*—almost verbatim to what I wrote in my phone. I thought it was a passive idea at best. I have about a million notes on my phone; each one is a quick blurb or quip about a story. Some have a few sentences, while others are as simple as *guy fights zombie with a potato gun*. I have no premise, no story, and really no substance. So, this one, listed as *That Bird Story Idea* wasn't very descriptive. Then it all poured out.

I told my wife about the idea once she came out of the store. She said my imagination runs a mile a minute, and who knows where these ideas come from. Thankfully, my brain does work overtime. It's a blessing and a curse, really.

Déjà

Sherry surveyed the vehicle's interior. Her vision was still blurred from the impact. Her first thought was of the children. It was always of the children. Her head felt warm. Blood rushed toward her head as she remained suspended upside down in her seat. Her positioning may have been the only thing to save her life, she thought. The shattered flecks of glass that had splintered from the windshield littered the space below her. Even if she disengaged the safety belt to try to leave, she'd likely hurt herself or injure the children. Sherry considered waiting for the rescue teams.

Tommy and Emily were secured in their car seats by the grace of God. Sherry thought about that phrase for a moment before doing her best to twist around to face the kids. A sharp, jolting pain struck her on her right side. Sherry glanced down, wincing in pain. A piece of debris from the car ahead jutted from her ribcage. It explained the labored breathing, she thought.

The kids remained unresponsive as she did her best to call out to them. Thomas stirred slightly but offered no retort. Sherry turned her head to check Emily, who was just out of her eyeline. The vehicle was silent, save for settling metal or fluids dripping from the undercarriage. She never felt more alone as the quiet of the outside world created a more unsettling environment by the minute. Sherry glanced into what remained of the rearview mirror, hoping to catch a glimpse of her children or would-be rescuer.

Moments felt like hours as she felt more hopeless and helpless than ever before. No Good Samaritan passerby to remove her from the carnage nor a saintly bicyclist to withdraw her kids from the devastation. It seemed to her nobody was coming. Her emotions took her over when she smelled a distinct odor.

"That's gas!" Sherry exclaimed.

The fireball erupted from the steering column in slow motion, engulfing the dashboard and console controls, then billowed from the climate control vents. Sherry could only watch in horror as the outside world disappeared beyond a wall of flames. She reached for her seatbelt once more but was unable to remove the buckle. Her lungs were pained, but she mustered a final primal scream as the flames crept over her body.

Sherry shot up in bed, screaming.

"Jesus Christ, what is it?" Tom asked, flipping on the bedside lamp, and discovered his wife sobbing, shaking, and dripping with sweat.

She motioned to extinguish flames off her skin, still unsure where she was.

As if instinctually, he threw his arms around her to console his wife. "Are you okay?"

Sherry finally calmed down enough to catch her breath, still clenching the right side of her ribs. "I don't know."

Tom sat upright in bed and threw on his tank top. "Well, if we're up this early, we may as well have coffee."

Sherry nodded and followed him to the kitchen, her gait uneasy and cumbersome.

Tom sat across from Sherry as the Keurig warmed up. "You look like you've seen a ghost. Want to talk about it?"

Sherry eyed the yellowed lights of the stove vent and at the faint morning daybreak creeping in through the blinds. She was safe, but something still didn't feel right.

"It's okay if you don't want to."

"No, it's fine. It just felt real is all," Sherry replied.

The coffeemaker filled the first cup, startling Sherry with the sudden hiss and sputter.

"I'll grab your cup first. Go ahead and tell me, especially before the kids figure out we're up at this hour. They'll want waffles," Tom said as he withdrew the cup from the machine. "Mostly Tommy."

Sherry smirked at the comment. Her son was a waffle fiend. If he was within a mile of a Waffle House, he'd smell it out. He was like a bloodhound for the doughy delights, even at five years old.

Tom slid her cup toward her and produced the milk and sugar before returning to prepare a cup for himself. The world outside was coming to life, with the songbirds chirping in the distance.

"Tom, it was horrible," Sherry said, her voice shaking. "There was this car accident, and the kids—"

"The kids are fine, honey," Tom assured while pressing Start on the coffeemaker.

"It felt so real, though. I still feel like my skin is on fire and like the piece of metal is still stuck in me."

Tom paused, unsure of what to say next. He wanted to carefully choose his next words, as to not seem patronizing or to downplay her experience.

"The worst part was that I couldn't help our babies, Tom. Nothing worked. I was trapped!"

Tom withdrew his cup from the machine and joined his wife at the breakfast nook. "I totally understand that, but the kids are fine, Sher. They're upstairs, fast asleep. At least for now."

Almost on cue, footsteps erupted from upstairs. The discord coming from the second floor only meant one thing to the parents.

"The kids are more than okay. They're awake." Tom took a sip of coffee.

Tommy and Emily barreled around the corner from the bottom step and bounded to the kitchen.

"Waffles!" Tommy yelled.

"*Waaaaaffflleeess!*" Emily sang out.

Tom gave his wife a sarcastic smile, as if to say, *I told you so.*

"I guess you better appease the natives before they become restless," Sherry said and set the table with plates.

Tom checked the clock, which flashed *12:00.* "Hon, can you fix the microwave clock in a bit? Stupid thing is blinking again, and you know how I am with that."

Sherry laughed as she placed a plate on the table. "You'd roll over for Skynet if it was real, wouldn't you?"

Tom whisked the waffle batter in a bowl. "In a heartbeat. All hail my robot overlords!" Tom preheated the pans for bacon and eggs, the obvious accompaniment to waffles. The waffle maker signaled it was warm, and he poured the batter.

Sherry helped pull the ingredients from the fridge and placed the eggs and bacon on the counter for him. Something felt off. She couldn't put her finger on it, though.

Tom jokingly flipped the eggs in the pan, showing off for the children's amusement. They giggled with every flip and cackled at every egg bit that spilled to the floor.

"Tom, someone is going to have to clean—" Sherry doubled over in pain, clutching at her ribs. This wasn't phantom pain from a dream. This felt real.

Tom rushed to her side. "What's wrong? Are you okay?"

Sherry slumped to the floor and rested against the kitchen island. After a moment, she couldn't move any longer. Every voice in the room became an echoed, disembodied blur. Nothing made sense, and the world felt upside down. She scrunched her eyes tightly to regain control of her sight. She opened them and glanced at the stove. Something wasn't right. She sniffed but couldn't smell the sweet aroma of waffles or maple bacon. "That's gas!"

The stove burners erupted in a belch of flames, engulfing the upper cabinets, and spread toward the breakfast nook. The flames were as real as they were hot. Sherry's face warmed by the second.

Tom panicked and attempted to reach for the extinguisher near the trashcan. His efforts were too late, as the fire exploded from the stove into the kitchen and dining area. The flames surrounded Tom and roared overhead toward Tommy and Emily.

"Jesus Fucking Christ!" Sherry shouted into a dark room.

"What? What's going on?" Tom asked groggily, reaching for the bedside light.

Sherry shook and shivered, shaking the feel of burning flesh from her skin.

"Damn. My clock is out. Let me check my phone. What time is it?" Tom reached for his cellphone on his home office desk. "Eight a.m.? We need to get the kids to school!"

Sherry looked at him in panic. All thoughts of the nightmare vanished, knowing the kids had to be leave.

"Get the kids up and ready. I'll get their lunches and take them." Sherry threw on a gym shirt and some old sweats. "Mommy's slumming it today. They'll deal with it."

Like a well-oiled machine, the two split up to get the kids ready, packed, and at the front door for their commute to school.

"Bye, Daddy! Love you," Emily said, wrapping her arms around her father, then climbed into her car seat.

"Bye, Daddy! Can we have waffles later?" Tommy asked as Tom buckled him.

Tom tussled his son's hair. "Sure, when you get home, bud."

Sherry backed out of the driveway in a hurry, waving to Tom in the driveway. The red light at Sixth and Pleasant Street was out. Sherry looked both ways before crossing the intersection.

"Mommy, are you and Daddy okay?" Emily asked.

Sherry glanced at Emily's reflection in the rearview mirror, then refocused on the road. "Yeah, honey. Why?"

"You seem like you saw'd a scary movie."

Sherry paused. "What makes you say that?"

"Well, Mommy, the truck crossing the street right now is about to hit us, and I think you hit it before."

Sherry glanced back into the mirror. "The what, now? What did you say?"

The impact struck the front driver's side with such force that the car tumbled several times before landing on its roof. The only sound Sherry heard was pipes clattering to the ground. As the car rocked to a halt, Sherry blacked out.

Vu

Ever feel like you've done the same thing repeatedly? Ever feel like you've done the same thing repeatedly? Well, that's where Sherry was in this story. I had a lot of fun writing a story like this, and it's been especially fun to involve entire families. It's a huge shift from *Spooky Tales and Scary Things 1*, where I had young adults and, at best, a father and daughter.

This was something I wrote for a creative writing course at a community college. One of the assignments was to write a story that spanned a certain number of words and had a beginning, a middle, and an end. As someone who specializes in all three of those things most of the time, this was an easy project. I got cracking and wrote a traumatic story for poor Sherry and the kids.

Some feedback from my professor was "Why does the kid like waffles? Is this even relevant?" Dude, yes. When I shared the story with friends, they said, "I relate to the waffle kid." It added a human element to the whole thing, and friends who had kids immediately connected with this dynamic. Not bad for a guy who doesn't have kids, right?

Much like the other stories in this book, I wrote them for class. I debated whether to include them in a spooky story collection because they're not "spooky." Like hell, they aren't! Imagine being a parent and repeatedly reliving the same accident, explosion, and the death of your family. That's pretty hellish to me. Much like "Connecting" and "The Shed," this story dealt with an infinite loop. While they're all drastically different in storytelling, the underlying theme was the same.

I got a 70 percent on the assignment. I hope you all enjoyed my 70-percent-grade story. Especially the part with the waffles. Specifically, the waffles.

The Monster on the Cover

I knew nobody would believe me. How was I supposed to confront a world that viewed me as inhuman? Am I destined for a path of destruction, or can one truly steer the ship toward their fate? Was I the captain of this ship of destiny, or was I merely tied to the bow, slowly drowning in seawater?

"Sir, they're ready for you on set," a young man called into my room.

I took a deep breath to calm my nerves. This wasn't my first rodeo; that was for sure. I'd had some incidents and happenstances that I could walk my way out of. If there was one thing I was good at, it was talking. My mother always called me the world's best bullshit artist. When I think about it, Mother was the only one who could see through my fabricated lies.

I dabbed more foundation powder onto the scar just above my eye. The impact had caused my eyebrow to have a missing patch, making it far more noticeable. I never wanted a makeup team to touch my face. The scar was far too large and not one of my proudest moments. It was a constant reminder of when I was a weaker man.

I can recall the event as if it played on a projector in front of me.
*****

I was sitting in the study while Martha did her best to care for the boys. They were playing make-believe, likely cowboys, Indians, or space monsters. I didn't care, as I was nose deep in my work. I was a financial manager for a big company, whom I will not disclose, as they wouldn't like me mentioning their name. I had just managed to balance the books and had brought us into black—a joyous occasion for any financial officer, for sure.

Martha entered the room, surveying my clutter with disgust and dismay.

"I'll sort this out this weekend. Promise," I said, eyeing the file folders and binders that littered my makeshift office.

She frowned. "This is why I don't like it when you take your work home, dear. It gets in the way. Go play with your boys, will you?"

I looked up from my ledger. "Do you know what I've done? This will probably put me on the map and give me a promotion. I'll be able to take you and the kids on that trip to the Keys, like we've been talking about."

Martha's face relaxed. "Okay, but you better wrap it up before dinner." She smiled and sashayed away seductively, as she did when making a point that I was too disconnected.

I resumed organizing everything, ensuring my papers were in order for Monday's impromptu meeting. She always knew how to rip my mind away from work.

The boys crashed through the door a few moments later. One dressed as a ninja, the other as a pirate. I wasn't sure of the correlation between the two, but I figured it begged asking.

"Since when did pirates fight ninjas?" I asked playfully.

Timothy spoke first. "Since ever, Dad!"

Richie echoed, "Yeah, Dad. Ever!"

Richie dove at Tim with his cutlass and knocked over a perfectly stacked pile of ledger books.

"Damnit, boys! What was that about?" I asked as books and papers rushed across the floor in a flutter. "What have I told you about horsing around in this office while I'm working?"

The boys looked somber and apologetic. "Sorry, Dad." They grabbed the documents to restack them.

"Just get off. I'll get them. Go bother your mother for a bit. I'll play with you two soon."

The two boys nodded and rushed off. Richie returned to grab his eyepatch before backing slowly through the door, then closed it behind him. I was finally hit with a wave of peace and quiet. Returning to my ledger, I penned the final figures into the blocks and closed it, with a satisfying grin. I knew this was big. This would be the day to change my life forever.

Slowly and neatly, I placed the binders into my briefcase, prepared for the meeting I would be the king of tomorrow. I could imagine how great the feeling would be—the attaboys, the firm handshakes vigorously quaking my entire body as they shook. I could take the boys to see the world! If not the world, we could at least start with Disney World.

I spent the better part of the hour daydreaming and thinking. Each new thought postponed my packing of the books. Eventually, I managed to put away everything and prepared for Monday. I didn't want to leave anything to chance. I brushed any fur from Moxi, our Labrador, from my Homberg before placing it perfectly atop the case. I would look dapper as I killed it; that was certain.

As I slipped into another daydream of how the day would play out, I smelled something that didn't seem right. I sniffed again, this time with more attention to detail. My heart felt like it had stopped in my chest. Smoke!

I ripped open the door, not caring if ten-foot flames were behind it. I needed to get Martha and the boys out of the house. Smoke filled the living area with a thick haze that made it hard to see. With quick thinking, I dashed into my office to look for something to cover my face. Reaching around on my coat rack, I found my cashmere scarf from Bloomingdales that Martha had gotten for me, several birthdays ago. I looped it around my neck once and bundled it into my hand, covering my nose and mouth as best as it could. It was thick enough to do the job. Like a madman, I dashed into the living room, calling for my family, as I crept under the billowing smoke.

"Martha! Martha!" I screamed into the clouds of noxious toxins. "Rich! Tim! Boys!"

Silence met my cries into the void. No voice responded. My veins stiffened with fear as I pushed toward the bedrooms. I needed to get the boys to safety. I passed the hallway to the kitchen, noticing the wall of flames already engulfing the walkway. The boys' room seemed untouched and pure as I approached. Soot stained the walls, but the door remained untainted.

I rapped loudly on the wood. "Boys! You in there?"

Rich's muffled voice replied, "Dad!"

"Hang on. I'll get this door opened! Step back!"

Without hesitation, I thrust my foot into the door and quickly broke it from the hinges. I never dreamed I would have the strength to break a door off its hinges, but adrenaline can make a man into a God.

"Come on. Grab my shirt, and don't let go. Where is your brother?"

"I dunno. Timmy was helping Mom in the kitchen like she asked and didn't come back!"

I did my best to give Richie an affirmative expression that conveyed how everything would be okay. I tussled his hair, and he gripped the corner of my shirt. The two of us crouched through waves of smoke toward the living room. I found the front door in the confusion and thrust it open. Smoke rushed toward the door to escape, stinging my eyes.

"Listen. I need you to run across the street to the Magerts, okay?"

Richie nodded.

"Tell them to call the fire department, if they haven't already. Stay there. Do not come back here. Got it?"

After another nod and a giant hug, my youngest dashed across the street like a lunatic and bound onto the opposite curb.

I refocused on the flames engulfing the living room, spreading from the hallway. I pushed past furniture and family photos that had fallen into the torrent of heat. The scarf must have been at its limits for smoke as I coughed through it. My eyes stung with smoke as I tried to cry out once more.

"Martha! Tim!" I heard nothing but a barking sound. "Moxi! Girl! Where are you?"

Barking sounds filled the air over the crackle of flame. I pushed closer to the sound, drawing myself into the thickest of the fire. There in the back doorway, Moxi stood, bounding in place and barking.

"Mox! Hang on!" I leaped over the collapsed grandfather clock in the hallway. I grabbed the back door handle and watched the smoke rush past as I swung open the door.

Moxi dashed outside for a moment, then back in. She barked like mad.

"What is it, girl?" I asked, realizing how silly it sounded.

Moxi barked a few more times, whimpered, then kneeled in the kitchen entry just out of reach of flames.

"Good girl, Mox!" I grabbed her collar to move her toward the door, but she didn't budge. "Mox, go!" I pointed to the back door, but she refused.

Moxi ripped away from me, leaving my fingers sore from her collar. She dove over the now charred China cabinet, its former beauty unrecognizable. The dog disappeared into the mysterious room I once knew as the kitchen.

"Goddammit, dog!"

I went outside for a quick breath of fresh air. A much-needed burst of oxygen reset my lungs enough so I could proceed. I rushed through the smoke, crawled over the China cabinet, stepped on the expensive dishes that Martha's mother had left to us after she passed, and landed firmly on the linoleum floor of the kitchen.

"Martha! Are you here?" I cried out.

I felt movement beside me. Something gripped my leg and waist.

"Tim!" I grabbed him quickly. "Where is Mommy?"

Tim pointed to the stove area. Flames and debris filled the corner. The cabinetry had collapsed from the wall, creating a disaster of rubble below, and pinned my wife under the wreckage.

"Tim, I need you to be a big boy and help Daddy, okay?"

Tim nodded. We pulled wood and sheetrock off her body while Moxi barked incessantly behind us. The thick flames rose around the four of us. I could all but see the hands in front of me as I pulled and gripped material and tossed it aside.

"Dad!" Tim screamed beside me.

Before I could react, a piece of the decorative ceiling slat crashed between us. I looked up just in time to see the second piece drive itself right into my head. That was the last thing I remembered.

I came to with an oxygen mask secured to my face and a blanket covering me. I gazed at a strong-jawed, blue-eyed firefighter.

"Where is my family?" I asked, realizing I could barely speak. My throat felt raw from the smoke.

"Calm down, Mr. Reynolds. You're going to the hospital for smoke inhalation."

"My family?" I cried out again and attempted to lift myself off the gurney, but the restraints worked well.

I attempted to cry out once more, except I passed out again ...

*****

"Sir, three minutes until airtime," the junior assistant called out.

I snapped back into reality, rubbing the scar on my forehead from where the falling ceiling debris had clobbered it. I took a deep breath and forced myself to follow the assistant to the main stage. Music played, and the audience cheered.

"Ladies and gentlemen, here to discuss his heroics and tragedies from his latest book, *Fire and Family*, please welcome author David Reynolds!"

The crowd whooped as I walked out. I scanned the nameless faces that filled the stands. The show's hostess carried a shit-eating grin, as if this was a show about animal adoption or overcoming obesity.

I sat in the chair, gazing once more into the audience. In the front row, my youngest son but now a teenager, Richard, sat with his girl-friend, Amelia. Every face aside from Rich was a stranger. As the show host prattled on, I did my best to answer questions, yet every response felt empty, and I felt numb. My feelings only returned when they displayed photos of the incident and of my wife's burns. The only unburned parts of her and Timothy were those where my hands and where my back had shielded them before the ceiling blow had knocked me unconscious.

As I answered questions, I felt more like a monster. *New York Times Bestseller* felt like an insult to me. I simply told my story—the tale of a man, who had discovered a financial loophole that never saw the light of day, turned hero. I wasn't a hero. I wasn't a savior. I was a failure. I was a monster, and I had the scars to prove it.

The Blurb on the Back

Much like other stories in this collection, I wrote this for class. The prompt was to write a short story involving a scar. Everyone else wrote about physical scars. They told stories about knife fights, battles, and violence. Obviously, I have no issue with that (see *Memoirs of a Crazed Mind*), but everything has its place. It got tiring to peer review story after story about dismemberments and murders.

I opted to write one about PTSD and mental trauma scarring. Of course, just to ensure I got full credit and that the professor didn't ding points if it wasn't obvious enough, the main character has a small scar above his eyebrow. This was another tale that sort of evolved into what you just read. I like when they do that.

"The Monster on the Cover" was a story about a guy dealing with a scar. One thing I enjoy is to write timeless stories. This one could have happened in any decade until the end. The children, the names, and the characters' actions felt like this could have been 1950s, 1990s, or today. One of my favorite parts to write is the time ambiguity.

It dawned on me that the plot would shift to the housefire only *as* I wrote it. I decided one of the children would go for help, and I wouldn't kill the family dog (see the name on the front cover isn't Stephen King.) I do like to give the sense of danger though, and one day I'll catch you off guard and obliterate the family gerbil or something. I ultimately decided the husband would be in peril while trying to rescue his wife and son, leaving their situation unknown due to the ceiling knocking out the protagonist.

The second half of the story is where the title comes from. Picture a book cover for the story about this guy's trials. He likely wrote a survivor story; his face is on the cover. He's not scarred or burned. He's relatively okay, save for the cut on his eyebrow. Fun sidebar about the cut on the eyebrow, too. When I was in the fifth grade, my classmates bet me five bucks that I wouldn't cut off some of my eyebrow hair with our art class safety scissors. It grows back, right? Best five bucks I ever made. And if you're wondering what that result was, look at any of my author headshots or photos, and you'll see the noticeable scar on my left eyebrow. I digress.

The big gut punch was that this wasn't just weeks or months later. This guy wrote the book likely fifteen to twenty years after the events. His now grown son sat in the audience. I love to beg the question: Did he do all he could? Does the son know how much he had tried to save everyone? Is the son feeling hate or anger toward Dad because of his failure? Or does he support him? He could be in the audience out of spite or out of love. Hard to say.

In the end, this was a fun story that I turned in for class, and I got a whopping 94 percent for a grade. I didn't write the story to fit the word count, unfortunately. So, sue me. I did my best!

Dewey

The library was quiet, and the listless world was as expected. Each book was a window into the world, and I was their keeper. Our branch was the first to consider overnight shift work within the county, possibly the state. I was their ambassador, a pioneer in the empty library's wilderness. For an introvert like me, the solitude among this many literary worlds was absolute bliss.

I scanned the first large stack of returns from the consistently ignored deposit box, pushing through classics like *The Great Gatsby* and *Oedipus*—a clear sign that a student had been through here. Somone had withdrawn several of Stephen King's latest novels in succession, possibly from a patron who had binged every story we had in stock. The podcast I was listening to malfunctioned briefly as I thoughtlessly pushed through endless stacks of unscanned books. It was odd to have such digital technology fail with a squelch, as if radio waves passing by dispelled the signal. I tended to my phone to restart the application. As I swiped through my phone, I noticed a figure pass down an aisle from the corner of my eye.

My heart raced. I considered dialing the police department, but that felt rash. Imagine my face when a late-working fellow librarian found themselves face-to-face with authorities. I shook off the notion that it was an intruder and took several deep breaths to work up my courage. I was, after all, a librarian. I passed the latest releases that someone had artistically strewn around a circular wooden table just in front of the checkout area and carefully navigated several carts of books and other obstacles in my path. I passed the cookbook section signage and crept by the how-to books. I heard light shuffling as I approached Classic Fiction. I reached deep down to collect the fortitude to round the corner and accost this trespasser, although I was at a loss as to how I would do it. Freezing in place, I counted softly in my head. *One. Two ...*

Three.

I whirled around the endcap of werewolf novels into the aisle. I felt uneasy, off balance, and shaken. I had not expected to see a figure standing before me. Part of me wished it was my imagination, that I had simply mistaken my poor eyesight or the glare in my glasses.

Here, standing before me, was a figure I felt I had seen before. A pale, light glow emanated from the man. It wasn't enough to illuminate, only creating an eerie backdrop for his translucent body.

"Oh, dear me! You startled the ever daylights of me, child," the man said, placing a book back onto my shelf and still appearing ethereal.

I trembled. "Wh–who are you?"

"Poe, clearly. Edgar, as I am affectionately known by friends and enemies."

I stepped backward. I was either sleep deprived, viewing a hallucination due to an exhausted brain, or I was in the presence of confirmation of the afterlife. "Are you...?"

"Dead? What is dead, truly, but another step in our existence. Were any of us truly alive?" Poe quipped, as if I should have already known the answer.

I swallowed hard before beginning a deluge of questions to confirm what my mind had already decided. My last question was, "May I touch you?"

My hand pressed forward before Mr. Poe replied, passing clear through his translucent upper biceps.

"Are we content?"

I nodded and stumbled backward slightly to find an oversized leather chair cradling me. We had developed a cozy reading area for our patrons. As Poe neared me, the fireplace kicked on, jumpstarting my already startled heart.

"Fear not. I come here often, as it quenches my thirst for knowledge and to be around a human comfort, such as the written text." Poe sat in the chair across from me. "I've not seen the likes of you before—a living soul wandering these corridors of literacy. I became insane, with long intervals of horrible sanity. Finally, someone to ease the passage of time."

"I just started here this evening. It seems I'll be here nightly." I fished for the words to say. "Are you in need of a friend?"

Poe scoffed. "Friends? I need not friends. How can one need a friend when they find themselves plagued by so many?"

My brows furrowed as I tried to understand what he meant. Was he talking about the day shift? Or about the patrons who filled the aisles daily? Before I could ask for clarification, several figures emerged from other aisleways. I pressed myself into the armchair, digging my nails into the tough leather. I darted my gaze between Poe and the others. Some looked annoyed that we were conversing, while others were elated about my presence.

Two stepped forward and took a slight bow.

"How do you do? I am Sinclair. Upton Sinclair. This lad next to me is Thomas," spoke the well-dressed, slick-haired ghost.

Thomas stood forward, looking all too familiar. "You can call me Tom. Or Mr. Clancy. However you'd like. Pleased to meet you."

The night progressed with pleasantries, introductions, and wild stories. As the day broke, my audience of the undead saw themselves out, fading from my view. I sat, contemplating what had transpired through the night, then resumed scanning books. I worked the night shift for another forty years before finding myself unable to continue. My only hope was to find my spirit wandering the library's aisles, as my new friends had done so many times before.

Decimal System

First off, I'd like to ask everyone, who the hell has never heard of the Dewey Decimal System? This story was another school assignment, and I got a lot of feedback about its name. Nobody had ever heard of the Dewey Decimal System. I remember one of my feedback items was "Dewey, like something that's been wetted?" Even writing that hurt my soul.

I thought it'd be fun for an overnight librarian to end up talking to literary greats. It's obviously set in Maryland, since every literary artist in the story is from there, including myself. Picture the excitement of having deep conversations with them every night, exchanging ideas and sharing a one-of-a-kind experience. All just by stocking books overnight.

I had a few librarian friends dig the story. It was good enough for me if they enjoyed it. They weren't my target demographic, but they were the subject. If they're not taking issue with anything, then I'm good to go.

Unfortunately, I don't have much more to discuss about its inspiration or backstory. Could you picture sitting down and speaking with an author or artist you've loved? Maybe a musician from the past? Oh, to dream!

Dream a Little Dream

Daniel knew he'd seen this woman before—something about her figure, the contour of her face, those eyes. He'd never forget those eyes. Piercing green, like a lost emerald hidden in a forgotten king's treasure room. He stared, mouth agape. One part of him wished he knew to look away, the other glad his awkwardness sparked conversation.

Before he could turn his head, she caught a glimpse of him.

"Can I help you with something?" the young woman asked, pushing silky brown hair from in front of her face.

Daniel shook as his leg bounced under the table, terrified about the next step. He froze, quietly cursing himself for not speaking up.

"Sir? Wait, do I know you? I feel I've seen you before. Did you go to West Central High School? Class of oh-eight?"

"No, can't say I did. I've lived in Oregon all my life. Never heard of that school before. I went to Lakeview."

The woman approached his table and sat across from him. "I know that I know you!" She tapped her finger on her lip. "Have you ever worked at Kroger's? Or maybe Tony's Diner on Fifth and Main?"

Daniel blushed slightly. His eyes widened as the memory of where he knew this woman from flooded over him like a tsunami. He'd seen this woman a dozen times, if not more. He knew every inch of her body. He knew her favorite books, movies, and even the fact that she disliked cherry cheesecake. This confrontation in the booth of his favorite restaurant felt uneasy yet strangely comfortable.

The familiar brunette relaxed in the booth, tongue in cheek. "Do you work on cars?"

Daniel shook his head. With each probing question, the answer was no. The more she asked, the more Daniel blushed. He knew he would have to say something. He'd have to reach deep inside for the strength to confess, to reveal how he had seen her every single night for the past four years. Daniel would need to come clean.

"This is just bizarre, right? Like, I feel like I know you. You're a Packers fan, right?"

Daniel nodded affirmatively for once.

Her face lit up with joy as she giggled slightly. "Okay, that was fun. I think you like Green Lantern more than Batman, yeah?"

Daniel smiled as he nodded. "Batman is—"

"Overrated!" she blurted out before he could finish, causing Daniel to smile.

The conversation and guesswork put Daniel at ease. They discussed the chance of meeting at the restaurant and sharing their interests, which made them both smile. The joy and happiness as they tried guessing the other's favorite interest seemed to only connect the two further.

Daniel found the courage to confess something as the conversation dwindled. "I know some facts about you, Lisa. I know you hate cherry cheesecake, the movie *Grease*, and despise the band the Weeknd."

The brunette's expression quickly shifted, as she appeared visibly shaken. "I never told you my name was Lisa, Dan."

Daniel leaned forward, taking her hand in his. For some reason, she allowed it. "Lisa, I've been dreaming about you for the last four years. We've shared adventures, stories, interests, and more together. Yet I cannot think of a time when I've ever met you. I feel like I already know your touch, only touching you physically for the first time today."

Lisa looked at her hand in his. She should have immediately withdrawn from him, but the touch felt all too familiar. The smell of his cologne triggered a sense of calm. She confirmed Daniel was indeed the man she'd been seeing every night when she slept. The two shared a bond that they could not explain. This was the very same man who had been talking to her, who had been dining with her, and who had spent so many great moments with her, even if it were a fantasy in her head. Today confirmed it was not an illusion but rather a shared dream. This sealed the deal. He was the one.

Lisa leaned over the booth and kissed Daniel's cheek.

He clasped her other hand with his.

The waitress returned with the bill, as the two sank into their chairs. "I do love seeing young ones in love. Love at first sight, it seems?"

Lisa looked long and hard at Daniel. "No, I think we've been in love for some time."

Years passed. Daniel and Lisa had shared their story with countless friends, family members, and coworkers. When I played with them at the park for my first soccer game, it reminded me of the time when they had shared a dream there years ago, which is the most exciting part of their love story.

They had collectively dreamed of their own child years before my arrival. They're gone now, but my parents had handed down the most extraordinary love story ever foretold to their son.

Perchance to Dream

This was yet another school assignment. Honestly, with all of it, I thought, 'Heck, this could maybe work for a short story collection, like *Spooky Tales and Scary Things*.' I enjoy the theories of shared dreams and fate. The fact that this couple had been "dating" in their dreams for ages made the physical meetup slightly awkward and that much more rewarding.

I think the fact that they both wanted to establish that the dreams had, in fact, been real was paramount. They knew so much about each other already, which was borderline stalkerish. I did want to change things up and have the tension ease little by little. At first, the guy is staring at her from across the restaurant. This sets up for a *who knows where this is going* scenario. I like those.

I liked dabbling in the idea of soulmates. These two were bonded in life and in dreams. They found each other through multiple planes of existence. Imagine being that connected? While it wasn't a spooky story, I wanted to end on a happy note. The ending, when I reveal the narrator, was my *ooooh* moment.

The child they had dreamt about was now grown up and retelling the story to others. Maybe this was among friends or at a gathering. Sadly, this could have also been at a funeral. I left that open-ended, but in either case, the parents dreaming about playing with their child, ten years prior, also opens the window to an afterlife-type deal. Maybe like that movie *Soul*? Maybe a connection exists between this couple and a spirit who eventually became their child, since spirits always exist? There are also inklings of clairvoyance too. Maybe they could tell the future?

All in all, "Dream a Little Dream" was a passion topic of mine to explore and a unique tale in my book, without conflicts or monsters yet still dealing with multiple levels of freaky stuff, like interdimensional communication or the afterlife. I hope everyone enjoyed it. What was your takeaway from this story?

Afterthoughts by the Author

I haven't necessarily run out of personal experiences to fictionalize. I'll never run out of those, so long as I keep doing things. *Spooky Tales and Scary Things 3* became a bigger-than-life idea, as I churned out tons of short stories during the 2020 pandemic and in class. I hope it was received positively.

I want to thank everyone again for the inspirations, likenesses, and more. I appreciate all of you and your misadventures. You guys gave me a lot of material to work with, from leaf-blowing lunatics to warning labels. Thank you for that.

I also want to thank everyone who has supported me throughout the past several years of my writing. It seems like only yesterday when everyone was reading my book, full of grammar and spelling errors. I didn't know what to do or how to get going.

I look at where I am today and realize I still have no idea what I'm doing, but I'll keep going. I have an editor to correct any issues that I may have missed. I have a great cover designer when I'm feeling less than creative.

Please support me by reviewing my books on Amazon, Goodreads, or on any of the big-box bookstores' websites. Go into the customer service area and request my books! Come pop by my table at a convention or a festival and tell me about your favorite story of mine! These things really can bring up a day, I'll tell you. I truly appreciate every one of you out there!

Stay spooky!
~ Harry

About The Author

Photo by Rick Currier

Harry Carpenter is an author born in Baltimore, Maryland. Sometimes they call that "Bawlmer," where he's from. He's a huge fan of video games, 80s movies and 90s Rock. Some of his favorites are playing Mortal Kombat and Doom, and watching Ghostbusters and Big Trouble in Little China while listening to Smashing Pumpkins and Chevelle. When he's not wasting time playing Xbox, he's writing some wild horror, science fiction and thriller stories. Some of his short stories have won awards! Harry is a huge fan of putting himself as the main character in most of his books, most noticeably in FUBAR, with the protagonist mirroring his thoughts and feelings while in the United States Army, which took him all around the world. Harry now lives in Baltimore with his wife and cats.

Follow Harry at www.hcarpenterwriter.com

Other Books by Harry Carpenter

In this series:
  Spooky Tales and Scary Things
  Spooky Tales and Scary Things 2

  The FUBAR sci-fi horror series:
  Fubar: Blackout
  Fubar: Out of Element
  Fubar: Situation Normal

  Serial Killer Thrillers:
  Memoirs of a Crazed Mind
  Chemical Burns
  Nightmares Unbound

9 789898 859109